THE OFFICIAL NOVELIZATION

CHRISTIAN FRANCIS

BASED ON THE SCREENPLAY BY LARRY COHEN

ISBN 978-1-916582-76-7 (paperback)
ISBN 978-1-916582-74-3 (ebook)

visit: echohorror.com

Contents

Adaptation Note

This novelization is based solely on the original unfilmed screenplay and not the completed film.

This is not the *Maniac Cop 3* that you have seen before!

Chapter 1

New York, 1990

In the Lower East Side of Manhattan, many streets within Alphabet City lay in ruin, its skyline filled with the bones of abandoned buildings. Their hollow frames were exposed, with the glass from the windows long since shattered. The once-proud businesses that had thrived here were long gone, and any old signage that remained was blotted out with copious layers of graffiti.

By day, it was a place in limbo, some blocks alive with music and the sounds of life, whereas others were eerily silent, where only stray dogs and junkies wandered. When the sun had set, like that night, hustlers, dealers and prostitutes came out to ply their trades freely on some of the more broken, trash-strewn streets and alleyways. But it wasn't entirely deserted. Between the vacant lots and crumbling tenements, clusters of social housing projects stood, their windows glowing against the dirty streets. The impoverished living as best they could.

The only businesses that remained were neon-lit liquor, gun, and sex stores, along with a copious number of pawnbrokers there to pay little for what people gave up in desperation as well as cater to those who didn't want to be seen by others.

Cutting through the silence of some of the abandoned evening streets, a pair of police sirens screamed past. These two vehicles sped through this part of the city, traversing the blocks at a frantic pace, with red lights blinking as they shot by.

Outside Ozzie's Hardware Surplus, one of the few honest stores left operating in the area, lay a blanket of glass shards. Having fallen from the smashed window at the store's front, the shards littered the sidewalk and street in front of it.

In the center of this dusk-tinted street, among the glittering of shattered glass and debris, a female body lay twisted in an unnatural, grotesque lump. The glow of the nearby streetlights flickered on as the night approached, casting long shadows over her, highlighting the obscene breaks across her skin.

Her head had been wrenched around a full one hundred eighty degrees, and her glassy eyes stared out blankly. The violence did not stop at her neck, though; her pelvis had been crushed. So had her ribs, which had been violently smashed until her chest collapsed inward, snapping bones and ripping through skin and flesh. Her whole body was contorted in a spiral of blood and shattered bones. The clothes she wore were soaked red and mostly torn off in the brutality inflicted upon her.

Every major joint was twisted at an extreme angle, cracked in the opposite direction. One arm sprawled limply across her chest as the other cracked upward, both being wrenched from their sockets, the skin around the joints split and bleeding. Each finger had been splayed out, snapped at opposing angles.

Her face was frozen in an expression of silent agony. Her mouth hung wide and askew. Blood smeared in thick, dark patches from out of her mouth and nose and dripped onto the asphalt below. Her once-beautiful features were turned into a picture of suffering.

The street she lay in was still, save for the distant sirens that approached.

Officer Teresa Mallory had been mauled and attacked in a way no human hands should be able to manage.

But she was not yet dead.

The police cars came hurtling out of a side street and skidded to a stop as all four officers jumped out with their guns drawn, cautiously circling toward her body, keeping their aims level and their eyes covering their surroundings, in case of anyone laying in wait.

One of the officers noticed the broken chainsaw

lying in the gutter nearby. "What happened here?" he exclaimed loudly.

"Quick," another shouted as he checked Teresa's pulse. "Call an ambulance! She's still alive!"

Within minutes, the ambulance had pulled up.

"What the hell?" one paramedic said as he crouched next to Teresa and surveyed her mangled body. "How is this possible?"

"I got a pulse," the second medic confirmed. "We need morphine, or she won't make the journey."

"Five milligrams?" the first asked.

Nodding, the second added, "If after thirty seconds she is fine, then push another five."

Quickly and expertly, the drugs were administered. Getting a gurney from the back of the ambulance, they started to lift her broken body onto it. As they did, an unmarked police vehicle pulled up.

From the driver's side, Detective Lieutenant Stan Moonjean stepped out. A large imposing man, he was built like an NFL player. With the darkest brown of skin offset with the palest of blue eyes, he was striking to look at. He was an imposing man who carried a haunted look of someone who had seen too much. He immediately saw Teresa's body on the gurney and rushed over.

One of the officers standing by saw him approach. "Detective? We were expecting McKinney."

"He'll be here . . . I'm not on this case," Moonjean replied, keeping his worried eyes on Teresa. "I was on stakeout two blocks away. I heard it called in."

The first medic turned to him, shaking his head. "It's not looking good. I wouldn't place a bet on her making it out of the street, let alone to the hospital."

Moonjean didn't look impressed. "Place a bet? You know who she is, don't you? She's one of ours!" He shot the medic an annoyed glance as he stepped over to the gurney. He looked down sadly at the mangled Teresa and could see no visible signs of life. "Hey, Teresa," he said softly. "It's Moonjean. Keep listening to my voice and hang on, okay? Fight with everything you got!"

As the ambulance sped down the street, Moonjean was sitting in the back, accompanying Teresa to the hospital. Detective Lieutenant McKinney had arrived on the scene and mentioned another victim that was found down the road, another female police officer who was almost murdered. He mentioned that the person who did it was a man they had dubbed the Maniac Cop. Moonjean didn't know what to do with that information. He was at the St. Patrick's day parade when the Maniac Cop struck, had been on a few of the murder cases before, and knew first hand what that maniac cop was capable of. He had even smelled his stench at some of the crime scenes. But he was involved in a racketeering case, so he did not get involved in this investigation. He was here for Teresa and would do everything possible to keep her from losing the battle she was currently locked into . . . the battle against the dark.

As a cop, Moonjean was tough, but he had no bravado about him. He just sat in the ambulance, holding Teresa's cold and limp hand in his, while the second medic kept working on her, trying his best to ease her pain as the ambulance rocked in motion.

The siren blared, and the lights flashed as the first medic drove at full speed down the road. The cars in front quickly veered aside to make room.

"Where are we going?" Moonjean asked the medic in the back with him.

"Queen of Mercy," he replied. "It's the nearest with a trauma unit. About five minutes away."

"You hear that, Teresa?" Moonjean said, leaning closer to her. "Stay with us just a bit longer. I'm holding your hand tight and not letting go." He looked up and noticed the medic eyeing him curiously. "I knew her old man," Moonjean explained. "I rode with him for my first years on the force. He wasn't too sure about having a Black partner . . . until he met me. Then he hated the idea . . . He was one hell of a racist bastard." He chuckled sadly as he remembered. "But despite that, I was proud to be his partner 'cause he was honest. Asshole or not. And her? I used to take her on some ride-alongs when she was thinking of joining the force."

Not sure why he was being told this. The medic

tried to veer the conversation. "Can you call him, tell him about her?" he asked as he moved over and strapped an oxygen mask carefully to Teresa's face.

"Nah, he's gone," Moonjean explained. "Killed at a gas station holdup. But he managed to take a couple of the bastards with him. He did his best. Don't think she has anyone. An aunt on the west coast, I think."

Teresa did not hear these words. She was alive but trapped in her unconsciousness. Despite her open eyes, she did not see through them. The only thing in her mind was the repeating images of what she had just gone through.

The stolen taxi ride.
The crash.
Matthew Cordell.
The broken window.
The chainsaw.
The unrelenting attack.

"I'm losing her," the medic said loudly as her vitals beeped loudly on the monitors, her heart rate climbing faster and faster, her blood pressure skyrocketing.

Moonjean looked down at her, meeting her blank stare. "You listen to me, okay? You are not some kind of weak cop who will let a few broken bones stop you! Now, keep holding on. If you see any shadows coming in, you tell them to fuck the hell off. You ain't done with life yet, and life ain't done with you. You get me?"

Out the front of the ambulance's windshield, the huge outline of Queen of Mercy Hospital came into view. This area of the city was no better than the streets where Teresa had been found.

What was once a modern building within a gentrified neighborhood had been turning into an antiquated relic in the middle of a grid of streets where junkies lined the pavement in varied stages of oblivion and gangs had created a battleground among themselves. This large hospital was a decrepit oasis slap-bang in the middle of urban decay.

As it drove up the long road to the entrance, the ambulance passed scores of gangs clustered on corners, selling weapons and drugs, junkies rambling up the street in a zombie state and the destitute asleep in alleyways. Residents of this urban jungle stared at the passing ambulance with disinterested gazes as it drove by. There was no sorrow or compassion on their faces. They were beyond feeling, only invested in their addictions or delusions.

A steepled church sat across from the hospital. Once an edifice of God now abandoned. Its front walls were almost entirely covered in graffiti. The building had been locked up tight, boarding all the windows and doors on the ground floor. And because they could not get into the building, the steps out front had become a sleeping place for the homeless or high. It was the ghost of a church in the ghost of a neighborhood.

The NYPD called this part of town the "Community Of the Living Dead," or C.O.L.D. There were so many places across New York City that had been abandoned and left to rot, but around this hospital, the danger felt more palpable. The tensions on the street always high, which made policing here nearly impossible. When one crack den was shut down, the junkies found another. When one gang was busted, the imbalance of power with rivals threatened a war. A war which could hurt innocents. So, they were all left to their own devices. It was unspoken, but the general NYPD thought was to leave COLD to itself. If any of its violence or drugs crossed into the lives of the innocent, then they would intervene; otherwise, there was not enough manpower to clean up these streets.

Through the high metal-barred gates, the driveway led straight to the emergency room receiving area. The ambulance had pulled up, the gurney with Teresa's broken body being wheeled in through the entrance doors, to where a medical team had been alerted and waited.

Moonjean escorted them in and said to one of the doctors. "Do what you can for her."

The doctor naturally nodded, though he could promise no more. He looked down at Teresa and, like everyone else, wondered how in the world she still had a pulse. How she was not screaming in agony. How she was even breathing.

The next hours crawled by for the surgeons who fought to keep her alive. From the spinal surgery, where she lay face down on the operating table, to realigning her shattered neck. Everything was delicately and cautiously worked on.

Doctor Peter Myerson, aged in his early forties, was a hotshot neurosurgeon that had already fallen foul of the ethics board. Having taken risks on patients and lost the gamble each time, his phenomenal skills were not enough to avoid the plateau his career took. Forced out of the more expensive medical centers, he had found the only hospital willing to hire him, despite the open medical investigation into past cases. But he was a pragmatist. He would serve his time here and refine his skills. What better way to learn than in the middle of a war zone? with endless surgeries from gunshots, knife attacks, and suicide attempts. Then, once he had been cleared of charges, he would make his way west to Cedars-Sinai in Los Angeles, where a job was waiting for him, a job he had told no one about. But it did not happen fast. He was in his third year of waiting to be cleared.

As he stared at the cracked bone through the open incision on Teresa's neck, Peter knew it was going to be a long, long operation.

Fifteen days later, after a dozen surgeries, he stood in Teresa's room on the intensive care ward and looked at her chart. He did not look too impressed by the latest readings and results.

Across from him, Detective Lieutenant Moonjean waited, having been sitting there already for an hour.

"So, Doc," he asked, "she's been the same for a week. You think she can pull out of this?"

Peter spoke without looking up from the chart. "Not exactly, no."

"What does that mean?"

Sighing, Peter replaced the chart at the end of Teresa's bed and turned to Moonjean. He spoke with a heavy, clinical tone. "She has no detectable cognitive brain functions. The most recent EEG confirms a complete lack of cortical activity. No awareness, no ability to perceive or respond to stimuli. Her brainstem is still regulating basic autonomic processes, which is why she can continue to breathe with the assistance of a ventilator. However, without life support, her body would not sustain itself." He hesitated before continuing. "At this point, medically speaking, there is no chance of meaningful recovery. While her heart continues to beat and machines maintain her functions, there's no consciousness, no ability to think, feel or experience the world around her." Peter let the words settle in the silence, giving Moonjean time to process this stark reality.

"So, she's brain-dead?"

Peter nodded. "In Layman's terms, I guess. And, unfortunately, it's irreversible. But she *is* alive."

Moonjean turned to look at Teresa. Unlike when she was brought in, she looked peaceful, with all her limbs back in their place. Her eyes were closed, her skin cleaned of blood smears. Her arms and legs were all bandaged, with metal braces setting the cracked bones.

"How long would you say she had?"

"With a heart as strong as hers," Peter replied, "she could live a long time."

Moonjean nodded. "At least they got the guy who did this."

"Was it that maniac cop, like the news said?"

"Yeah. Broke into Sing Sing and got burned up like a marshmallow. Fucker deserved no less."

"Do they know why yet?" Peter asked. He wasn't really interested, but he was polite enough to keep the conversation going. "Wasn't there some issue with his identity? I saw something on TV . . ."

With a shrug, Moonjean then rubbed his eyes. "First, we thought it was a cop, a guy called Cordell. Then they said it was this serial killer pretending to be him . . . But I don't fucking know. Seems no one can keep the story straight." He glanced at Teresa again. "Lot of good it does her anyway. No matter who did it, she is still here."

The next two years passed over New York City like a blur.

Life carried on.

The name Matthew Cordell drifted from collective memory, and the nightmares the Maniac Cop wrought were simply a record in the history books. One that plainly stated that the killer's name was, in fact, Stephen Turkell.

For the policemen who had seen the Maniac Cop, they knew this story was a lie. Turkell was a tiny, wiry weasel of a man, not the juggernaut they had seen or heard about. They knew it had to be Matthew Cordell, but no one could bring themselves to question it out loud.

From St. Raymond's Cemetery, the buildings beyond its perimeter resembled much larger illuminated tombstones, rising above the other gravestones that littered the lawn.

Matthew Cordell

1942–1976

Rest Eternally

The headstone inscription listed the year he died in prison. Not the date a decade later, when he walked around as a walking corpse, taking bullet after bullet, murdering innocent people for his twisted revenge against a city that wronged him. No, Turkell was blamed, and Cordell was cleared of all wrongdoing. His soul and body were laid to rest.

His grave, though, was not like the others here. It had been crudely disturbed, with mounds of dirt tossed in all directions, not as if someone had dug anything up and left neat piles but as if something had dug their way out.

Splintered shards of coffin wood jutted up through the earth, peeking out past the grass line and down in the hole, the box that held the remains of Cordell emptied.

The Triborough Bridge stretched across the dark waters of the East River, linking Queens, Manhattan, and the Bronx. Below it, the waters churned lazily as its black surface reflected the winking red aviation lights on top of the bridge's towers.

The hum of vehicle engines reverberated against the metal as a steady stream of taxis, delivery trucks, and weary late-night travelers pushed on with their journey.

The tollbooths, each manned by NYPD officers, were small glassed-in stations. They flickered under fluorescent lights that made the officers inside look almost spectral. Most motorists chose to pass through the automatic exact-change gates, hurling their coins with a clatter as they advanced in a single file. Some, though, chose to pay with bills at the one manned booth on duty.

There, where the fluorescent strip light inside the booth was broken, a toll cop sat in shadow. A brand-new Porsche roared as it approached, coming to a quick stop at the barrier. Behind the driver's seat, Tony

Morcalino sat. A typical affluent, overdressed trust-fund kid. Barely twenty, he was seated beside a beautiful woman, Tina, who was not with him for his brash attitude or spoiled nature.

Winding down the window, Tony thrust a hundred-dollar bill toward the cop without even looking up to offer any greeting or pleasantry.

From within the booth, a dirty, white-gloved hand reached out and accepted the offered bill.

Tony's hand remained extended, waiting for change.

But it did not come.

"What's with this guy?" he smirked, turning to his girlfriend. "Too busy to do his job?"

Tina chuckled. "What can you expect from a guy who does *this* for a living?"

Tony still didn't even have the decency to look at the cop in the booth as he addressed him. "I expect change from a hundred, you know? Don't even think to shortchange me."

"Maybe he doesn't speak English," Tina said. "They hire a lot of immigrants now."

Tony nodded in agreement. "Yeah, all kinds of idiots become cops. There's no goddamn standards anymore." With his arm still hanging out the window, he clicked his fingers impatiently. "Hey, I'm waiting here. Let's go! Let's go!"

A honk from the car behind made Tony even more agitated. "Hurry the fuck up, you—"

His words turned into a pained, shrill scream as he jerked his arm back into the car. His eyes went wide in shock, and he fell against his seat, passing out as blood sprayed over the inside of the Porsche.

Tina screamed louder when she saw his hand was missing—chopped off at the wrist. Arterial spray covered them both as Tony slumped, dying, while all of his blood pumped out in spurts. His pressure dropped with each beat.

The cars behind them still honked impatiently, oblivious to what was happening. The sounds of terror were lost among the roar of passing engines and horns.

In the booth with the broken light, only the shadows remained. The dirty-gloved officer was gone.

Chapter 2

The prison ward of Queen of Mercy Hospital was a stark place. With every window barred and every door locked, the hallways were guarded twenty-four seven by armed officers. This was a section of the hospital where suspects would be brought if they had been seriously wounded during their arrest or during their time waiting for arraignment in one of the city jails. It was a continual conveyor belt of stabbing and gunshot wounds, where just over half of the patients survived.

Past the entrance door to one of the two patient rooms was a collection of a dozen beds. Basic. Impersonal. Cold. At the far end, a few private curtained cubicles stood.

Doctor Naomi Fowler was in the furthest of the cubicles, administering to one of her patients. She was changing the dressing on the man's chest, where a bullet from a .38 caliber gun had been pulled from his chest the day before.

Naomi tried to face each day and each patient with a sunny disposition and positive outlook. But in this, her fifth year covering the prison ward, she had little positivity left. Gone was her long hair, having opted for a buzz cut after one patient grabbing her by it in a drugged-up frenzy. Her clothes, too, were function over form. Thick black jeans and a plain shirt. Nothing revealing. Nothing sexy. Nothing grabbable. Her sunny smile had been replaced by a dark sense of humor laced with a mountain of sarcasm, her defense mechanism against this job. But she still loved her work. She loved helping, even if they called her a slut, a whore, and a bitch on a regular basis.

This patient was Frank Jessup. A violent brute of a man, cuffed by the legs and feet to his bed, with a wound that, despite the medication, agonized him.

"Why couldn't you just let me die?" he grimaced in a wheeze as Sarah tied the bandage off.

"Don't give me all the credit," she said with a dry smirk. "Your body is one tough SOB. It doesn't wanna die quite yet, even if you want to."

"You saved me—and for what?" he asked with a glare of resentment. "They'll just send me down for life. Maybe transfer me outta state so they can gas me."

Naomi stood and walked around to the end of the bed, took a pen out of her lab coat pocket, and started to make notes on his chart. "Hey, you're breathing now, safe in bed. It could be worse."

Jessup wasn't listening. "When those assholes yelled for me to drop my piece . . . I thought to myself, you know what? Now it's fucking over. *Finally*. All those years trying to hide shit I did and all I had to do was point a fucking gun at them, and they'd do the rest? I'd have no questions. Wouldn't have to explain shit. And no punishment. I'd get out of this shit once and for all." He paused and smiled at what he was saying. "And when that slug hit me? I was fucking grateful. I was so numb I didn't even feel it hit. Just the darkness climbing up over me, then . . ."

Naomi was not affected by his words. She was made of much stronger stuff. "And then you opened those big brown eyes, and you saw my pretty face."

"Oh, fuck you, cunt!" Jessup cursed.

Putting his chart back on the end of the bed, she smiled. "Just for that, no lollipop for you!"

As Jessup screamed more obscenities at her, Naomi walked out of the cubicle, closed the curtains behind her, and was met with a waiting nurse. This was Buddy, a hulk of a man in his mid-twenties, overly sweaty and dressed in blue scrubs.

"That's what I like about you, Doc," Buddy said with a smile. "You don't let them get to you. You always keep a smile on your face."

"Well, if you don't smile, you'll probably just cry," she replied as they walked across the ward slowly.

"Oh, I got a new one to show you," he said, taking out a Polaroid from his pocket. "Female cop this time."

Naomi thought Buddy was a special kind of man. He had the body of a tank, the strength of a bear yet the temperament of a kitten—soft-spoken, almost child-like in his kindness. A gentle giant whom she enjoyed working with. She felt like he was a bit lost and needed guidance.

But he had a habit of taking photographs of patients throughout the hospital. Ones he liked to show to her with quiet reverence. He always said he took them because he liked to pray each morning and needed to look at their photographs to do it, that it helped him remember them. But something about it really unsettled her.

She had sworn to herself: next time he took an unwanted picture of a patient, she would tell someone, and she had told him about that, too.

Despite the warning, here he was, another Polaroid in hand.

The picture was of Teresa Mallory, unconscious, with many wires and tubes coming off her body.

"She's been on life support for nearly seven hundred days," he said, impressed. "Most people shrivel up when they're on there for that long. But she looks like she could just get up at any moment. She's pretty. I really like her."

Naomi glanced at the photo. "You got permission to take this?"

Buddy avoided the question. "I'll put her in my collection so I can pray for her along with the others."

"If you didn't, I'd have to tell someone. You remember that?"

Buddy didn't answer and just looked at the photo with a smile.

They passed a bed where a prisoner with his name tattooed on his head lay. Kenyon. With one leg amputated at the knee, he grinned lasciviously as Naomi looked at him. He then pulled back the bedsheet with his manacled hand, exposing his stumpy erection. "Hey, I'm growing me a new leg, Doc. Wanna check it out?"

Used to this kind of behavior, Naomi did not react and easily ignored the comment.

Walking out into the corridor, they headed to the locked security doors at the far end.

"I should put a catheter up him," Buddy mumbled. "That'll teach him a lesson."

"That's just his sense of humor," Naomi said, putting a hand on Buddy's shoulder. "Leave him alone, okay?"

As the guard at the security door saw her, he turned a key on his dashboard console and pressed a large green button. A sharp buzzer sounded around the corridor as the lock clicked open, and the first of the heavy doors swung open.

She stepped through into the short space before

the second door, then swiped her card over the sensor, unlocking it instantly.

They were in a public hospital, but in this ward, security was as tight as any prison.

The intensive care ward was filled with the sound of beeping monitors and hushed conversation as doctors milled about on their rounds and nurses, more or less, ran the place.

Getting off the elevator on the third floor Naomi walked over to the nurse's station, where Beechum, the head nurse, sat. A woman with an expression like granite and a demeanor to match. She glanced up and saw Naomi approaching with disinterest.

"Doctor," she asked. "What are you doing down here?"

Naomi sighed, not wanting to be here but seeing little other choice. "I thought you might like to know that one of our nurses has been snapping Polaroids of one of your comatose patients."

"Why don't you file a formal complaint?" Beechum asked. "He sounds like a creep."

"I'm not sure it's malicious, and I don't want to cost him his job," Naomi said, unsure. "He's just a bit . . . I dunno. Slow. I guess. He's harmless."

"Who was the photo of?"

"I'm not sure of her name, but she's a cop that's been on support for two years."

"Oh, yes, that's Officer Mallory . . . One of Doctor Myerson's. But he left early. I think he had a date." The nurse paused for a moment. "So, I guess it *is* over between you after all?" As she spoke, she relented with a wide smile. Her steely exterior had been merely an act for Naomi's benefit.

Naomi just laughed and shook her head. "It's so very much over between us."

"Well, I'll make a note to keep an eye out for any more amateur photographers, okay?" Beechum said. "How's the prison ward anyway? I'll never, for the life of me, know why you work up there."

"I have no idea, either. I mean, why do you do what you do? Why did that female cop do what she did? We could all be homemakers instead of all this bullshit, married to an asshole and drunk on wine by midday."

"Maybe we're just all control freaks?" Beechum shrugged. "Anyway, for Myerson's patient, I don't really think it matters that anyone took her picture. There's no family round here. No visitors ever come aside from some policemen now and then. She won't ever wake up to complain."

"Then, why is she being kept alive?"

"That's a question for your ex . . . You can go see her if you want, she's in 307."

"You know what?" Naomi replied. "Why not? I'm curious to see her chart. Must be a reason she's still hooked up." She turned to walk away but not before looking back at the nurse. "And can you not call him my ex as a personal favor?"

Beechum nodded, though having no inclination to do that.

As she moved down the corridor toward 307, the bustling sounds of the ward gradually faded around her, replaced by the muted beeps of monitors within the patients' rooms.

Getting to the door, Naomi noticed that it was already partially open. Pushing it, she entered. The lights inside were off, with the only illumination coming from the hospital's exterior lights that shone through the slats of the Venetian blinds, casting lined shadows across the room.

Naomi stared at the bed on the far side, hearing the *beep-beep, beep-beep, beep-beep* of her monitor. It was quite peaceful here but also very sad.

She did not see anything else in the room. She had no idea about the ominous shape in the far corner from her, away from the light through the blinds. An immense shadow that blended into the background. Only if someone stared long enough could they discern that a shape was there, a hulk of a figure with its head downward. This figure was also far enough away from Naomi that she did not smell the stench of death that permeated from it. A smell of filth mixed with rot, earth, and burned flesh.

Officer Teresa Mallory lay rigidly in bed with a multitude of tubes and cables, with electrodes placed over her body. The respirator hissed with each exhalation as it breathed the oxygen for her.

Wires ran from a matrix of sensors on her head, eventually leading to an EEG machine that showed the wave patterns of her brain. Wave patterns that were flatlined and had been since she was first admitted.

Grabbing her chart, she read a couple of pages in the moonlight. She read the litany of injuries she came in with. *That's why she is still here,* she thought. *Myerson doesn't know how she survived it.*

Stepping closer to the bed as she put the chart down, Naomi paused as her eyes caught the EEG waves suddenly changing. An increase in activity on the screen. She then turned and saw rapid eye movement under Teresa's closed lids.

"What the hell?" Naomi muttered quizzically.

She glanced once more at the EEG screen, examining the spiking waves once more. Her surprise was evident as she knew one thing: the diagnosis she had heard from the head nurse was incorrect. The patient's mind was not dead. Teresa's brain was very much active, even if not conscious.

She was too engrossed in her thoughts to notice the shape in the shadows had begun to loom nearer, out of the corner and slowly approaching. The beeping on the monitors imperceptibly began to speed up, though not enough to steal Naomi's attention. Teresa's heart rate was increasing, just as the shadowy figure moved closer.

Leaning forward, Naomi put her hand on Teresa's forehead. She felt very warm to the touch . . . too warm for someone unconscious on life support.

"Officer Mallory, can you hear my voice?" Naomi said. "I'm here beside you. My name is Doctor Fowler."

The shadowy thing drew even closer to the bed. A stained white glove reached up out of the darkness, toward Naomi.

Suddenly, Teresa's eyes flicked open as she stared up with a look of abject horror on her face.

Stunned, Naomi struggled to find the words. "I'm going to get help."

The gloved shape in the shadows then started to retreat away from the bed.

Naomi raced to the nurse's station, as she had no idea what was happening with the patient, but she felt as if she just witnessed a miracle of sorts.

Beechum glanced up from behind the counter as she approached, out of breath. "What's the matter?"

"You have to come with me," Naomi gasped.

"As soon as I finish—"

"No, right now!" Naomi cut in with a sharp urgency.

Getting up and walking around the counter, Beechum looked confused as Naomi led the way back to room 307.

"Is something wrong with the patient?" she asked.

Naomi smiled. "I've got a big surprise for you and for Myerson."

Getting to the door, Naomi gestured for the nurse to go in first, which she did, flipping on the light switch. The dimness of the room was chased away in an instant as the fluorescent light bathed them in a clinical, cold hue.

Teresa was in her bed as before. But she was not awake. Her eyes were closed as if they had never opened. Her expression was back to being blank. Returned to the deep trance she was in. The hisses of the respirator and beeps of the monitor were all as they were. The EEG waves were flat.

The rest of the room was empty otherwise. There was no dark shape.

Nurse Beechum examined the monitors, then turned to check Teresa's pulse, which seemed expectedly slow. "I don't see any change."

Naomi stood, staring at Teresa, trying to figure out what happened. "Her eyes opened. She looked *at* me," she said, almost questioning herself. "Her readings were really active."

"I doubt that," Beechum dismissed. "She has no possible prognosis that leaves her in any better condition than this." The nurse then looked at Naomi with concern. "Are you sure you are not just exhausted? It can get too much all these split shifts, you know?"

"I'm telling you it was an active alpha wave on the

monitor. She was dreaming, then she looked at me. Right at me!"

Beechum did not know how to respond. She knew what the monitor said and what the patient's pulse implied. "There's no indication of any of that now. Or from any of the past two years we've checked in on her."

The beeper on Beechum's belt sounded. Piercing the space between them with its high-pitched tone. Checking it, the nurse then walked toward the door, turning to look at Naomi before she left. "I have to go. You should probably go back to your ward."

"Can you make a note of what I saw in her chart? Whether you believe it or not. And I'll talk to Myerson tomorrow."

Beechum nodded. "I hope, for your sake, you did see that. Otherwise, you need to take some time off. Can't have you going all screwy now, can we?"

Naomi smiled in return. "Can't argue with that." Taking one last look at Teresa, her expression slipped a bit as she thought, *I did see that . . . Didn't I?*

Naomi Fowler clocked off from her long shift, still slightly shaken by what she saw in room 307. She walked down the front steps of the hospital, her footsteps clacking with an echo with each step, and she felt the bite of the chill outside. The dawn was not yet here as the night shrouded everything.

To her left stood the old wing of the hospital, trapped in mid-demolition. Two of its walls had been torn away, leaving levels on the verge of collapse. It was a frame of a building, nothing more than a stripped skeletal corpse. Its flesh long gone, with only brittle bones remaining.

Hurrying her pace toward the open parking lot next to the old wing, Naomi did not notice that the security post was empty.

As she walked toward her small car. Just a few yards in front, through the chain-link fence, another similar car was parked on the street. But unlike hers, that one had been completely stripped of parts and, like the old hospital wing, was a skeleton of what it once was.

As Naomi fiddled in her purse for her car keys, she heard a scraping of feet coming from her left. An unwelcome noise in this otherwise empty quiet.

A few rows of cars away, weaving their way in her direction, was a group of teenagers. Obviously, with gang affiliation, they looked high on some kind of drug. They laughed like hyenas as they tried to focus on their unsteady steps.

Quickly unlocking her car and praying to any God that would listen, Naomi got behind the wheel and immediately locked the door.

Only a few seconds later, two of the gang stood outside, leering in. "Hey lady," one said, staring into the window, groping for the door handle. "Wanna party with us?"

Without waiting, Naomi turned on the ignition, hit reverse, and slammed on the gas, narrowly missing the men.

She backed up through the parking lot with speed, moving her car down the aisle. Behind her, the drugged-up gang gave chase.

Her car barely slowed down as she reversed her way through the gates and into the street before skidding the vehicle around the right way.

"Aw, don't be like that!" one of the gang shouted out as they came to a stop by the road, too tired to continue the chase.

Avoiding an oncoming vehicle, Naomi turned the wheel sharply and straightened the car up. She passed the steepled graffiti-covered church and sped off down toward her home in Queens.

She did not see that the side entrance to the abandoned church had been broken into. The large board, torn off, lay in shreds on the ground.

Inside the church, very little light found its way beyond the broken entrance. The pews that used to fill the room were piled up at one end. The large stone altar, stripped bare. Even the once stunning marble floors now lay cracked and filthy, overgrown with moss.

And in this dark, sitting on the steps leading up to

the altar, was a man. Motionless. Almost frozen in place, he could have been mistaken for some piece of statuary that had been left behind. Cloaked and hidden, the large man sat, dressed in a dirty, moldy and burnt police uniform.

A man who did not sleep.

A man who simply waited.

Matthew Cordell.

Elsewhere, also caught in a state between life and death, Teresa Mallory lay in her hospital bed.

Chapter 3

The next day arrived uneventfully. Outside the Queen of Mercy Hospital, the regular mix of lost souls and the desperate came out to find their latest fix as gangs resumed their pitches on street corners.

Inside the hospital cafeteria, Doctor Peter Myerson was walking along the food line, picking out a small salad and a sandwich from the selection and placing them on his tray. He looked like he hadn't slept and was not really paying attention as he moved to the end of the line and was met by the smiling face of Doctor Naomi Fowler. She held two coffee cups and placed one of them on his tray.

"Black and two sugars," she said. "Just as you like your men. I remember it well."

Peter could not help but smile. "Hi, Naomi . . . I heard you were looking for me?"

"Yeah, did you read Beechum's report?"

Peter sighed and shook his head. "You expect me to believe that? There is physically and medically zero chance that what you thought you saw happened. No way at all." He nodded to a free table by the window that overlooked the parking lot. "You wanna join me?"

With a thin smile, not liking what she saw being so easily dismissed, Naomi followed him over to the table and sat.

"You know me better than that, Peter," she said, keeping her voice low. "I'm not imagining it. I saw it."

Peter took a sip of his coffee. "Are you saying there's no way that you could be mistaken about this?"

"The woman opened her eyes and looked *right* at me. I'm telling you." Naomi struggled to keep her volume low and out of the earshot of other staff here. "Her EEG was going ballistic. Like crazily so."

"Let's just assume that science forgot what it was for a while and what you say happened happened. Okay? You really shouldn't be telling me this."

"Who, then?"

"The Ethics Committee is meeting tomorrow to decide if they're going to pull her off support." He unwrapped the sandwich as his tone became maudlin. "They say that you can't put a price on a human life. But the money guys think that she isn't worth the six hundred thousand dollars a year to keep alive. So, Ethics stepped in, and they are gonna side with the money . . . just as they always do."

"They can't do that!" Naomi said loudly, catching the ears of surrounding tables.

"Actually, legally, they can." Peter shrugged. "Her next of kin—an aunt, I think—gave full permission to this hospital over a year ago." He took a bite from his sandwich.

"Can you oppose it?"

He had to wait a moment to speak as he swallowed his mouthful. "'Cause of my record, I don't have a say . . . I kept her alive all this time, against all medical odds. It's a miracle she survived. And we have no idea how or why. But at least I saved her, even if they decide it's better that I didn't."

Naomi thought for a few seconds. "What time tomorrow?"

Peter's brow furrowed. "Naomi, please stay out of this. If you go in there saying she woke up, when we have all the tests and results saying she can't, you're going to blow any credibility you have with them." He paused for a beat. "Why do you always look for ways to sabotage your career anyway? Did you catch that from me?"

Naomi sighed. "Really? It's a woman's life. Even if she won't ever recover."

"Hey, I agree. I'm not the bad guy here." Watching Naomi get up from the table, Peter offered a smile, knowing that he couldn't say a thing to settle her mind. "Thanks for the coffee."

. . .

A brand-new Mercedes 280SL, with less than two hundred kilometers on the clock, tore through the night, weaving through the streets close to the hospital. Behind the wheel, two privileged female trust-fund brats reveled in their reckless ride. High on cocaine, they took turns topping up their nose from a tiny gold spoon that the passenger held with a giggle.

Trying to aim her spoon to the driver's nose as the car swerved, she spilled it all over their lap instead. As she did, they both broke into uproarious laughter, barely even looking ahead and missing a collision with a parked car by a gnat's hair.

Further ahead, a derelict pushed his trolley full of old clothes and cans across the road. Paying his surroundings little mind, he did not even hear the Mercedes approaching as it smashed into his side.

His trolley went spinning, spilling its contents over the asphalt as his body launched over it.

The impact sent a loud *crunch* through the night as the Mercedes then careened wildly, tires screeching, before slamming head-on into a concrete wall. The Mercedes's windshield shattered instantly before raining the glass down over the hood. Its front grille crumpled inward, the force of the collision buckling the bumper with a howl of metal. As it did, both the headlights burst inward.

The derelict's body had come crashing down in the middle of the street. His leg splayed outward, shattered in multiple places, as he screamed in agony.

The driver's side door was quickly flung open, and the woman stumbled out, her designer, cocaine-covered dress having been ripped at the shoulder and a thin trickle of blood trailing down her forehead. She swayed unsteadily, heels scraping against the concrete, as she tried to orient herself through her high. A second later, the passenger got out from the other side, coughing, her trembling hand still clutching her tiny gold spoon.

Both of them staggered onto the street, dazed. The reality of what had just happened struggled to cut through their fog of drugs and adrenaline. The driver was more concerned with her car, not the man she hit.

"Jesus! Look at that," she complained. "That's a few thousand bucks minimum."

The passenger looked around at the streets and noticed that no one was coming out of the buildings. No one had heard them. "Babe, there's no witnesses," she urgently whispered. "Let's just get out of here!"

The derelict did not hear what was said. He only saw the women looking at the damage to the car. "Help me," he pleaded in a pained gasp. "Call an ambulance, please. The hospital's just down the block."

The driver shook her head angrily and turned to the man with no pity or care. "You dumb prick!" she said cruelly. "Look what you did to my fucking car!"

Coming from behind her, the derelict saw something that made him feel a sudden pang of relief, a police officer striding down the shadowy sidewalk toward them.

"Oh, thank you, Jesus," the man whimpered, gripping his broken leg as he tried to lessen the pain.

"Oh shit," the passenger soon whispered as she noticed the approaching officer, too.

In the partial shadows on the sidewalk, the policeman paused his approach and stood, staring at the women silently.

The derelict winced in agony as he spoke. "These assholes were gonna leave me here! They ran me over."

"No, no, we were just gonna find help!" The driver lied in a put-on innocent tone. "Honestly!"

"Yeah," the passenger agreed. "We were gonna."

The policeman did not reply. He was motionless.

"Why ain't ya moving?" the derelict cried out. "Arrest them!"

"We're not that strong," the driver said, playing the helpless female card. The only one she could think of to play. "If you could help him into our car. It's a bit smashed up, but I'm sure we can get him over to the hospital."

The policeman resumed his pace forward. Both the driver and the passenger took an unsure step backward, thinking that he was coming for them, but he walked straight by and over to the derelict. Through their still drugged-up state, they didn't notice his face or the condition of his moldy, burned uniform. Nor did they see his gnarled face. They just saw a blue blur go by. The driver did, however, manage to catch a waft of his rotten stench, and she almost gagged.

Walking straight over to the derelict's fallen shopping cart, the policeman picked it up by its metal frame and set it upright on its wheels. The policeman then walked over and scooped the derelict up in his huge arms then placed him in the shopping cart. The pain in his leg made the derelict cry out as his body slumped against the metal.

Unlike the women, the derelict clearly saw the officer's face and uniform. The missing nose. The one bulging and one sunken eye. The copious amount of healed but open wounds across his face. The rotten clothing. The shining police badge on his chest read *Cordell.*

"Help me?" he called out to the women.

The policeman didn't pause as he started to push the trolley along the road at a brisk pace. This was much to the amusement of the two coked-up women, who had to stop themselves from laughing out loud.

"What the hell are you?" the derelict screamed at Cordell in fear.

Before the man could ask anymore, Cordell glanced over the crest of the hill, down the other side, as the street ran straight toward a busy intersection. With an enormous force, he then pushed the cart forward, releasing it on a plummeting path.

The derelict screamed as much as he could, unable to control what was happening. The wheels on the cart turned furiously as it hurtled down the incline, picking up speed.

Cordell just stood, watching, as the cart got to the intersection. The cars honked as they swerved to avoid the derelict speeding into their lane. One vehicle could not avoid clipping the cart, sending it spinning like a pinball marble at a dizzying speed into the path of an oncoming truck. There was no chance for the derelict, whose screams were cut short. The truck slammed into him. Another car failed to avoid the collision as it slammed into the other side of the cart, crushing it and the man flat. Killing him in an instant. Crushed from either side, pulverizing as the grated metal of the cart sliced through flesh and bone, squeezing him through its small slats in a millisecond. The only part not crushed into a pulp was the top half of the derelict's head, from his nose upward.

It sat atop the crush, still attached by threads of skin and flesh within the ruined meat of the rest of him. His eyes still open and staring out.

The two women could not help walking after the cop in curiosity about what he did. They witnessed the cruelty of his actions and the fate of the derelict. They were frozen in terror, dreading the horror that could follow.

But he did not advance on them. He just turned as

if called by something, his head tilting slightly before he then resumed a brisk pace away down the sidewalk.

Harlem was a cultural haven for diverse ethnic communities. Life there was not always easy as crime and poverty held a firm grip, but there was pride. It bustled with the colorful mosaic of cultures, where African, Latino, Caribbean, Jewish, and many other peoples intertwined, each adding their own flavor to the streets. It was a place of resilience, of survival, where history clung to the brownstones and tenement buildings like the faded murals of Malcolm X and Celia Cruz that adorned some of the neighborhood's walls.

On one street, vendors lined the sidewalk, selling everything from knock-off designer handbags to stacks of Coltrane, Nas, and old Motown vinyls. The air was heavy with the scent of sizzling street food grills, empanadas crisping, kebabs charring, and the yeasty aroma of fresh bread from an all-night bodega. Conversations in Spanish, Creole, and patois mixed with the occasional outburst of laughter, a reminder that, for many here, Harlem was not just a home but a place where cultures were transplanted and, against the odds, took root.

Yet, just beyond this bustle, this culture, the decay of the city, crept in. On nearly every block, some tenements or storefronts were abandoned. Boarded up.

Their entrances were locked with rusted chains, their walls spray painted with tagging. Some buildings had even been totally removed from existence by demolition crews but were never built on. They lay as hollow areas where all had been razed and just existed in a decrepit limbo.

Detective Moonjean stepped off the curb, his eyes passing over on one such lot. A space where brick and mortar had once stood. The building that used to be there had long since been knocked down. In its place, a makeshift dumping ground where broken furniture, shattered glass, and discarded syringes mingled in the dirt. Fires flickered inside rusted trash cans, where the glow lit up the figures huddled around it. Their faces half-lit in the light.

He had asked each of them the same question but was met with a slurred shrug or the look of contempt. Him being a cop was one thing, him being a Black cop in a neighborhood that had been persecuted by the police in the past . . . was another thing entirely.

Moonjean expected that attitude, though. He was used to the derision. But when it all boiled down to it, he was a cop. He was here to protect. Even if they didn't want it. He prided himself on being an honest officer. Not that he wouldn't bend a law. He knew the system was broken, but he also knew what he had to do to make what he did count. Make his actions help and not hinder. If that meant roughhousing a suspect, fine. If it meant planting evidence to get rid of a suspect he knew to be guilty, fine. But he would never cross the line of his own morals.

"Two buildings over," one old drunk finally answered Moonjean as he weakly pointed to the east of the lot. "That lot's in there somewhere."

With a silent nod of thanks, Moonjean wandered further into the shadows, through a broken part of the wooden fencing, into a small alleyway leading between the buildings. After stepping over clumps of overgrown weeds and refuse, he soon saw the rear of the building in question.

With no electricity, only the glow of candles crept out of the dirty windows of the gutted house. Once quite opulent, it was now a ruined shell of its past.

Climbing in through its empty bay window, Moonjean made his way through, into the hallway. Without a flashlight, he relied on the small flickering candles that lined the hallway in front of him.

Weaving his way along the twisting narrow corridors, he soon heard the faint sound of drumming. Coming from the basement of the house. Slowly, he walked toward this tribal beat, following it down the rickety wooden steps into a basement. On each one, a candle burned over the remnants of the previous candle. Its wax dripping down, forming a solid splodge over the last.

The repetitive drumming sounded like a dreamy heartbeat, as the closer you got, the more it seemed to drag you toward it.

As he reached the bottom, he looked around the corridor ahead of him and felt as if he were at sea. The drums sounded a repetitive ebb and flow that made his mind sway as if it were caught on choppy waters. Steadying himself, he walked on until he reached what he came to find.

A Haitian ceremony was happening in the main sublevel room. At the far end, a Houngan, a Haitian high priest, stood. He was presiding over a ceremony with a steely glare across his small congregation. He wore a long robe in a deep shade of blue, embroidered along its edges with a multitude of golden Vévé symbols as well as intricate geometric patterns. The robe was cinched at the waist with a wide, woven sash of red, yellow, and green. Around his neck, dozens of beads and pakèt kongo charms clattered softly with every movement he made. On his head stood a towering, wide-brimmed hat wrapped in silks, adorned with bloodied rooster feathers. His thick white dreadlocks hung down from inside the hat, draping over his shoulders. He carried, in his dark and weathered hands, a gourd rattle, covered in beads and snake vertebrae which he shook, punctuating the rhythm of the drums.

The room itself was bright with orange candlelight as bowls of burning herbs infused the air.

Half a dozen people stood in front of the Houngan and chanted in unison, a deep wavering drone, which rose in pitch as the drums got louder. The drummer, meanwhile, sat naked in the corner, covered in hand-painted symbols and played as if he were in a trance. His eyes rolled back in his head as his hands beat the skins with precision.

Moonjean was the only one not caught up in the frenzy of the service. Nor did he look surprised, shocked, or even the slightest bit curious as to what was going on. He just stood patiently at the back. Waiting for the ceremony to end.

When it eventually did, after about twenty minutes of the same chanting, the small congregation filed out quietly, leaving the Priest staring at Moonjean with a knowing smile on his face.

"I never expected to see you again at one of these," the Houngan said.

Moonjean smiled. "You didn't make it easy. Took a while to find you."

"We need our privacy, keep the malandrens away, you know?" The Houngan walked up to Moonjean and placed a hand on his arm. "It is good to see you, my friend. I hope the Catholics are treating you well?"

Moonjean looked uncomfortable.

The Priest smiled. "It was the will of Bondye that you left. So, all is well between us."

"I'm glad."

"So, why are you here, then?"

"I have to ask you about zombies."

The Houngan's jaw clenched slightly. "What is it you want to know?"

"You remember that maniac cop?"

"He is dead, no?"

"This is why I had to speak to you. Anyone else I'd say this to would just laugh."

"There is nothing funny about the dead," the Priest grimly replied.

"I've been on a few cases over the last few weeks, and I think they're him . . . I don't think I'm wrong, he's a zombie."

The Houngan looked at Moonjean intently. Trying to figure things out. "Tell me . . . What do *you* know of zombies?"

"I . . . I never told anyone before but . . ."

The Houngan moved closer. "But?"

"I . . . saw one when I was eight years old." He took a deep breath in. "I was living across from Cimetière de la Rue Toussaint Louverture outside Pòtoprens."

The Houngan chuckled. "Now that's a resting place where there is little rest. The ground there is sour."

"I used to walk back from school through it . . . and I . . . I saw one."

"The zombie?"

Moonjean nodded with a forced smile as he tried to not get dragged down by his bad memories. "He was naked and so wrinkled. I was as close to it as I am to you and . . . I could smell it. *That* smell . . . Like death."

The Houngan watched Moonjean carefully as he rolled a wooden bead between his fingers. "So, you think this cop is the same?"

His voice was neutral, unreadable.

"That smell from Pòtoprens. I smelled it at the crime scenes," Moonjean said. "I smelled that kind of death."

"If that is what you smelled, then he was called," the Houngan said simply. "If you came to me for validation, there you have it."

"But what if he wasn't? What if he just came back?"

A flicker of something crossed the old man's face. It was gone just as quickly. "Everything follows a balance, Moonjean. Death has rules, just as life does. But sometimes . . . sometimes, the river flows in ways even the Loa do not expect." He turned slightly, extinguishing some of the candles around the room with his fingers.

Moonjean frowned. "You sound like you've seen it before."

The Houngan let out a small laugh, shaking his head. "I have seen *many* things, my friend. Not all of them should be spoken of." He turned from the candles to look at the detective. "You should be careful where you tread. The dead do not like to be disturbed."

Chapter 4

The hospital room's closet had laid empty for two years, until then. A policewoman's uniform hung alone on a single hanger, covered in a dry-cleaning bag, put in there by Father Paul.

This middle-aged Catholic Priest had a sagging face. Prematurely aged, yet he felt even older inside. He had served as a Priest in this hospital for many years, and seeing the constant procession of gang-on-gang violence, rapes, and murders took its toll. In a hospital like Queen of Mercy, you would see the worst of humanity in much greater numbers than the best of it.

In Teresa Mallory's room, he closed the closet door and sighed. It was a sad thing he had to do, bring the clothing for someone to be buried in. It was like giving up the fight before they were beaten.

A knock at the door stole his attention. Turning, he saw Detective Moonjean in the doorway.

"Father Paul?" Moonjean said. "What brings you here?"

"Stanley," the Priest smiled. "Part of my work is here at Queen of Mercy. I can't be at St. Paul's all the time." He motioned to Teresa with his hand. "Officer Mallory's family contacted the hospital. They asked her uniform be brought, in the event of . . ." He looked for the right words. "In the event she succumbs. And I volunteered to pick it up."

Walking in, Moonjean curled his lips and half-heartedly shrugged. He looked at Teresa sadly. "I'm surprised they even cared. Not like they have been here to see her even once."

"Grief shows itself in different forms, Stanley. Just because they have not been here does not mean that they are not in pain."

"I guess," he replied. Standing beside Teresa's bed, he looked sadly at her. "Do you think she's brain-dead, Father? Like totally gone?"

"Define death?" the father answered in a soft, even tone. "You see, with all the sciences man has discovered, we don't even know *what* death is. *Still*, we don't know. Sure, we know what physically happens to the body, but that is all we know. We have no idea how it all works." He paused. "So, sure, her brain may be 'dead' by scientific benchmarks, but that means little when you consider the presence of a soul. Perhaps that lives? Science cannot address the equation of the soul at all. Some say the body loses twenty-one grams upon death. Some say that the soul has no weight. Some even say that dreams are your soul imagining. But it's all best guess and faith. So, to answer your question, no, I do not believe she is gone. No one ever is."

"I guess we'll all find out someday, huh?" Moonjean mused. "Hopefully not for a long while yet, though. Not a question I'm that eager to find the answer for."

As he spoke, the Priest motioned to a necklace of charms around Moonjean's neck. "Is that what I think it is?"

"What do you think it is?"

"A voodoo Fetish?" the Priest said, looking quite shocked.

"It's just a lucky charm from my past, nothing more," he replied, feeling uncomfortable under the priest's scrutiny.

Quickly making his goodbyes, Moonjean then left the room. He intended to stay with Teresa for a while, updating her on everything, clinging to the futile hope that she might somehow still be able to hear him. But with the priest in her room, he thought it best to come back later, to save any more awkward questions about voodoo.

If it wasn't for Teresa, he would not come here at all. After her father died, he felt that someone should be there for her, even like this—because no one else was. So, he would swing by to talk every once in a while. It was as much company for her as therapy for him. He didn't really talk to many people, so he used his time with her to vent his emotions and frustrations. It was a mutually beneficial arrangement, even if she had no idea about it. That day, though, was not one of those days. She would need to wait until next time to hear his latest complaints.

As he walked down the corridor, Moonjean was quickly reminded about how much he hated hospitals. As he passed a sick patient slumped in a wheelchair, they emitted a hacking, lung-rattling cough. One that made Moonjean hold his breath as he walked by. It was so loud and sickly, and they didn't even cover their mouth . . . It made him feel nauseous.

Reaching the elevator, he pressed the call button with his elbow, determined to avoid touching anything with his hands, convinced the man's coughing had left germs everywhere.

As the doors slid open, he rushed inside, feeling some relief to be out of the corridor.

This was short lived as, almost immediately, he was followed by a nurse, wheeling the hacking patient in the wheelchair. Still coughing, still not covering their mouth.

On the first floor of the Queen of Mercy Hospital, were the administrative offices where all the non-medical staff worked, assistants, accounting, human resources, and administrators managing the day-to-day operations, ensuring everything ran smoothly.

Unlike the rest of the building that carried with it the smell of disinfectant, here, the air smelled faintly of coffee and printer ink.

In its large conference room beyond the cubicle offices, a dozen members of the hospital's ethics committee sat around a large circular table. Made up of senior doctors, attorneys, head administrators, and the hospital director, they were the ones who decided the fates of certain patients, not based on ethics as their name would suggest but who weighed up the hospital's liability against variables like public relations and legal liability.

A doctor could be brought in front of the committee as their actions may have been deemed unethical, but if there was a chance the board's decision could garner negative press attention or added costs, they altered what should be a moral decision to suit their needs better.

As an ethics committee, they were remarkably unethical.

They were debating the fate of Officer Teresa Mallory.

The hospital director, Kenneth Powers, was not a doctor. He was deemed a non-medical professional who was an administrator and business manager. He did not really understand the details of medicine but could see the bottom line. The cost. The variables of litigation. As a wealthy man in his sixties, he was always perfectly manicured, groomed, and dressed, a stark contrast to the exhausted and bedraggled state of the medical staff in this hospital.

Sitting at the far end of the table, Doctor Peter Myerson was in the middle of answering this committee's questions—at least he was trying to between Powers's hyperbolic statements.

"The old wing being condemned and torn down has caused an acute shortness of beds," Powers stated in a cold monotone. "And yet we're maintaining this patient in a chronic vegetative state at significant cost to the hospital and with little sign of a recovery."

One of the attorneys decided to add to this conversation. "I'm sure if the patient were competent to make the choice herself, she'd prefer to die."

"Thank you for your medical insight, Doctor," Peter said sarcastically to the attorney. "I don't think supposition without any actual facts should be any consideration here nor cost. It's about a human life. A *living* human life." Despite his natural bluster, after talking with Naomi, he felt that he had an obligation to fight for Teresa's life, even if he never saw a route of recovery for her.

Before he could carry on, a sharp rapping at the door stopped the conversation, and without waiting to be answered, Naomi stormed in. Wearing her white doctor's coat, glasses on, with an expression like she meant business.

"Doctor Fowler?" Powers said, not happy that anyone interrupted the session. "What are you doing here?"

"Apologies," she said, addressing the room. "But I have some information about Officer Mallory that I need to raise."

Powers paused as he glanced at Peter, then back to her. "Well, we are discussing that right now, but unfortunately, that is not your patient, Doctor. Nor any of your business."

"But I did witness significant activity on her monitor—"

Raising his palm to stop her mid-sentence, Powers said, "Doctor Myerson has told us all about that. And we all believe as a committee that it was in all likelihood a brief malfunction of the equipment. Nothing more."

"How does that explain her opening her eyes and looking at me?"

"Please!" Powers said dismissively. "There's no one to corroborate that claim of yours, and you're hardly an expert in the field of neurology. So, if you will excuse us. This is supposed to be a closed and confidential meeting."

Naomi turned to Peter. "Isn't there anything you can do to delay this?"

He did not look up to meet her gaze. He just spoke

while looking down at his papers in front of him. He couldn't fight anymore. He knew neither of them could win this. "Naomi, quality of life must be taken into account. And what is the quality if she is just alive because of our machines? It's not like she can talk or form any conscious thought."

Powers did not like Naomi's bluster. He did not like opposition in any form. He looked at her bitterly.

The ventilation ducts in the conference room were made of hollow metal. They snaked through the walls, carrying and filtering oxygen down to the basement below. The vents, positioned discreetly along the upper corners of the room, created an acoustic pathway, allowing voices to travel along the ducts with surprising clarity.

Unbeknownst to the committee seated around the round, polished table, their conversation was not confined to this room. It wasn't very private as deep in the basement, past the hospital's storage rooms and maintenance corridors, someone was listening.

Standing in the dimly lit space where the ventilation ducts opened into one of the sublevels, a figure was still, tuned to the faint but distinct voices that filtered down. The murmurs of discussion, pauses, sighs, even the subtle tension in certain words, reached this figure almost perfectly. In the shadows, they listened intently, piecing together every word, their presence unknown to those above.

Kenneth Powers's voice reverberated down to the

waiting ears of the large scarred, rotten figure. "Since we have permission from her next of kin and since we as a committee concur . . . a committee you are not part of Doctor Fowler . . . It has been decided that the patient will be removed from life support tomorrow morning. I shall be signing the documents at 9 a.m. sharp."

The meeting soon ended, and the committee dispersed.

Kenneth Powers was relieved it was over. That was his last order of business for the day, and he was glad to be making his way down through the radiology department to the exit.

This department, like some other wards, was closed after 6 p.m. A cost-saving measure Powers was proud to have implemented, even if it made the doctors' lives more stressful. More money equaled more profit. And for Powers, that was the bottom line. So, this closed ward was a good thing. Not to mention that it also gave him a private way to walk out of the building, with no people to bother him and no patients to look at.

He carried in his hand a slim briefcase and wore a long black trench coat, both items, of course, designer branded and cost more than any worker in this hospital could ever comfortably afford.

Powers's demeanor was intimidating, and to everyone who worked under him, he was feared . . .

And he knew it and liked it. It was only when on his own that the stern expression dropped.

As he walked through a set of double doors, passing a row of the X-ray rooms, he was lost in his own thoughts . . . But he was soon brought angrily to the present as a loud clatter of metal broke through the silence around him.

He stopped in his tracks. His thoughts immediately went to the idea that a doctor was here working when they shouldn't. Especially as the lights to the X-ray room that the sound came from were still on. More costs to the hospital.

Pushing the door open, he peered inside. "Who's here?" he asked, unimpressed. "This is a closed area. No one should be here." Looking around the bright room, he did not see anyone but on the floor lay a number of broken X-ray plates.

"For Christ's sake," he grimaced as he walked in to pick them up. "Whoever is here, come out *now*."

Powers always walked the same route from his office on the way home. He also always left the office at the same time, almost by the second. So, if anyone wanted to find him away from the throng of other staff, right then and there would be the time and place to do so.

And that is exactly why Powers was standing in this X-ray room, looking angry, unaware of how predictable and vulnerable he was at that moment.

With a loud smash, the door on the far side of the

room swung open. There in the brightness of the strip-lights, the rotten hulk Matthew Cordell strode in like a steamroller. His gloved hands outstretched as he lunged for the screaming hospital director.

Unable to avoid the Maniac Cop, Powers was seized around the throat and yanked off his feet. His briefcase fell to the floor as he was picked up and swung through the air. He twisted in Cordell's grip as he was then thrown down with a shattering thud onto the metal X-ray table.

Powers's head cracked audibly as it collided with the table, knocking him instantly unconscious.

The huge gloved hand then reached up, grabbed the X-ray generator hanging on a metal arm above them, then moved it over Powers's head.

Powers did not hear the machine being switched on nor the dial getting turned to maximum. Neither did he feel the generator above him start its scan nor hear the Maniac Cop leave the room, turning the lights off as he left.

For the first few moments that the machine scanned him, Powers's head began absorbing harmless amounts of radiation. But the moments turned to minutes, and he did not wake as the burning sensation started. By the time an hour had passed, the rays had penetrated into his deep tissue, with burns beginning to develop on his scalp and face. After three hours, he was still unconscious as his hair began to burn at the roots, and the burns on his face got deeper and more severe.

It was in the fifth hour that Kenneth Powers finally woke up to the terrible pain of what he was going through. Almost immediately as he screamed awake, his stomach contracted, and he vomited. Still on his back, staring upward, the matter ejected from his belly and spewed out of his mouth all over his face. He spluttered, trying to breathe, too weak to move. He could not see as his eyes had clouded over, but he could smell his own burning flesh.

With his brain swelling and suffering radiation necrosis, his thoughts were fast deteriorating. The skin on his face began to sag, threatening to slough off from his skull at any second.

He had left the office for the day without signing the order to terminate Teresa Mallory's life support.

Hours before the hospital administrator woke underneath the X-ray machine, Teresa Mallory was lying in her dark room. The glow from the exterior lights, once again, shone through the Venetian blinds, casting their slatted shadows over her and her life support.

She was not alone, though. Only moments before, the door had opened, and a large shadow moved in the room, closing the door behind it. It was Cordell. Seated in the darkest corner of the room, his gloved hands rested on his lap. He sat still, unnaturally so, for a couple of hours. Watching her. Waiting.

When the time came, he stood to his feet. Slowly, he began to take each of his gloves off. The stained and charred fabric came off to show his hands. Mottled with death, scarred by attack and blistered with fire. They were terrifyingly monstrous paws. Putting the gloves into his jacket pocket, Cordell then crossed the room, over to the immobile Teresa.

He reached out to her with one hand.

He simply touched her cheek gently. As he did so as his skin contacted hers, the brainwaves on the EEG machine spiked again.

He then raised his other hand to her other cheek and placed both on either side of her head. Her brain waves then went wild. Zigzagging in a fury.

She lay motionless in her hospital gown, wires still trailing from her arms, tubes winding up her face and into her nose and mouth.

The monitors beeped faster as her heart rate sped up and became more erratic. The respirator quickened its pace.

Something was happening.

Deep within Teresa's weakened mind, fragmented dreams flickered past her mind's eye. Distorted, unsteady, with their edges as blurred as fading memories.

She found herself standing in the middle of a barren landscape, a no-man's-land where, once, a city had thrived. Its towering skyscrapers of metal were now reduced to ruins. Torn down, razed to nothing but remnants of their former splendor. The ground, covered in a black sand, was strewn with the shattered remains of what had been. Twisted steel, broken glass, fragments of a world long lost.

A reddish haze hovered inches off the ground, swirling around her feet, licking up at her brilliantly white dress. Its fabric billowed around her like a cape as she started to walk forward. She knew she was looking for something, for someone, but her mind was a mass of confusion and uncertainty. She wondered for a moment, trying to remember why she was here, why she—

Then she saw him.

She knew who it was, even though he was without any mutilated features. There was Matthew Cordell. Tall. Powerful. Dressed in his crisp NYPD uniform. He was youthful and handsome. Not the monster she had seen nor the one who had put her in here. This was the man. The real man.

He smiled at her as she approached.

Time then slipped in this dreamscape, and within seconds, Teresa's lips were touching Cordell's. They were kissing passionately in each other's tight embrace.

Pulling her head back to look at him, her smile fell. There was the horribly scarred, rotten, and rancid creature she knew as the Maniac Cop. Even his moldy uniform was how she remembered it. The horrific stench. In this dream, though, instead of screaming and running from him, the opposite happened. She threw herself at the monster in all his putrid glory and began to kiss him even deeper. And he kissed her back, his blackened tongue jutting over his cracked lips and scarred mouth.

Her fingers brushed gently against the deep, criss-crossing scars on his cheeks.

As the clock struck midnight, Nurse Beechum began on her rounds of the intensive care ward. She had to go to each patient, check their vitals, and note them down on their charts, and doing this late at night was something she very much enjoyed doing. Mainly as none of the patients were awake, and she could do her work in relative peace without the polite chatter they all wanted to make.

Having checked on most of the patients, she walked along the corridor to the next room. 307. Teresa Mallory's room.

As she approached, she quickly noticed the door was shut.

She looked confused. She always left the patient doors open. No matter what, she never closed them. From all her time in the intensive care ward, she knew better than to cut off a patient. With doors closed, sounds were muffled—if they were heard at all and cries for help were more difficult to decipher.

She had not closed this door, nor was there anyone here who could have. She was the only staff member down here on the night shift.

Pushing the door partially open, she peered in. Not knowing what she was about to see.

Inside, the lights were off, and the glow through the blinds was dull.

The respirator and the life support monitor displays were bright, but unexpectedly, no *beeps* or *boops* could be heard coming from them.

Reaching in, she flipped the light switch.

Nothing. The room stayed dark.

Opening the door further, she stepped in. She soon felt something else with her in the room.

A panic rose within her. "Who's here?" she demanded with a tremble in her voice. "Answer me . . . You answer quickly, or I'm gonna start screaming."

At once, a huge scarred hand, shot out and grasped around her throat, stopping any possibility of her screaming.

In the rest of the ward, no patients were awake to hear the noise, and no doctors or nurses were on duty. No one heard even a scuffle of feet as Nurse Beechum was dragged from the room by her throat, her legs flailing as they tried to find purchase on the linoleum floor.

Down the corridor, this semi-conscious nurse

clawed at the hand that crushed her windpipe as it then wrenched her body up, toward the large laundry chute hatch.

The broken body of Nurse Beechum would be found in the morning soon after Kenneth Powers's charred and radioactive corpse. She would be found in a cart at the bottom of the laundry chute. Twisted and piled among the soiled towels, sheets, and pillow cases.

Even at night, the lighting in the prison ward was excessively bright—and deliberately so. The harsh fluorescent strip bulbs overhead cast an unyielding brightness that left no corner untouched. Shadows were eliminated as secrecy was stripped away.

This ward felt entirely separate from the rest of the hospital. With soundproof walls and thick, locked doors, nothing from the world could be heard within, and conversely, nothing inside could be heard outside.

In one of the single occupancy prison cells at the end of the corridor, a wild-eyed female patient struggled violently with Buddy, the male nurse. Her frail yet determined hands clutched tightly onto a tattered book. An old volume, with a brittle leather cover. One that was cracked and worn with age and threatened to fall apart in this frantic tug-of-war. The book's yellowed, speckled pages were already loose from their bindings as they started to spill onto the padded floor.

"Hey, what's the trouble?" Naomi asked as she appeared at the cell's doorway.

Buddy didn't even turn as he let go of his grip, then stood back. He stared at the patient, Felicia, as she clasped the book to her chest. "She's not allowed to keep this, and she knows it!"

Felicia shook her head. "No. That's a lie! They'd always let me keep it in the other wards."

Naomi stepped in. "What's so important about this book?"

"My mother gave it to me!" Felicia explained with hurt in her voice.

Buddy looked at Naomi with a smirk. "The same mother she hacked up and left around Brooklyn in plastic bags."

His words visibly shook Felicia. Not that the orderly was wrong, but her mental state was fragile at best dealing with all of this.

"I can take it from here, Buddy." Naomi smiled. "Can you go check on the wards for me? Make sure everyone is okay?"

With a shrug and a nod, Buddy left.

Naomi did not let her gaze leave Felicia, who, as soon as Buddy was out of sight, dropped to her hands and knees and frantically started to pick up the loose pages of the book that had fallen out. Grabbing them, one by one, she sorted each back into the volume by page number.

Naomi could see that it was a volume entitled *The Pentamerone or The Story of Stories*. "Is it a good book?" she asked in a kind tone.

"It's the first edition," Felicia said, unsure. "If it was in good shape, it would be worth thousands. That's why he wants to take it away from me. To try and sell it."

Naomi crouched and picked up a couple of pages from the floor. On one was the title page that said *Sun, Moon, and Talia* by Giambattista Basile. "Felicia, what is this story about?" she asked, handing the page back to her. Trying to engage her in some conversation. Trying to calm her.

Felicia had been transferred to this ward while waiting for sentencing. The other prisons were not equipped to handle inmates with severe psychiatric conditions, and she had been deemed too unstable for the general population. Her mind fractured by whatever was in her past and what made her what she was.

Naomi had seen cases like this before, fragile, teetering, needing care, not cruelty. Though she was not a psychologist, she needed to help her patients.

Felicia's fingers trembled as she took the brittle paper, not looking up as she spoke. "That story's the original sleeping beauty," she murmured.

"Like the cartoon?"

Felicia smirked, her demeanor lightening. "Not

like that. That's the watered-down version, not the original like this. This one would blow kids' minds."

"It would?"

Felicia nodded. "In the original, it's not Prince Charming but the king. And he doesn't kiss her to wake her up. He falls in love and basically rapes her while she's asleep."

"Okay, I was not expecting that," Naomi said with genuine surprise.

"Right?" Felicia chuckled, still sorting the fallen pages into number order. "Anyway, in the story, she doesn't even wake up from it. She gets pregnant with twins. She only wakes up after one of the babies suckles on her finger and sucks out a splinter, which removes the curse."

"What about the baby? Was it okay, if it ate the cursed splinter?"

Felicia thought for a moment, then nodded. "Yeah . . . You know I never thought of that. It's a bit of a plot hole," she laughed. "But that's not even the end. The king's wife then finds out and tries to kidnap the kids to eat them out of jealousy . . . It has a kind of happy ending, though. The king finds out, saves the day, then has his wife thrown into a fire. Then he marries the sleeping beauty, and their kids are fine."

"Wow," Naomi said, not sure if she believed this patient's story.

Having got her book back into order, Felicia moved

to the corner of the padded cell, still clutching it, and sat down. "Can I keep this?" she pleaded weakly.

"Yeah, don't worry." Naomi smiled. "You can keep it, anyway. I'll let everyone know, okay? Is there anything else I can do?"

Felicia looked up, hopeful. "Can I get one of those yellow pills? I want to sleep . . . I want to dream."

Naomi nodded. "Of course. I'll see what I can do."

Felicity closed her eyes in hope. "Maybe in my dreams, the king will show up with a hard-on for me too?"

Naomi chuckled. "Well, anything is possible."

An hour later, Naomi had finished her nightly rounds. She was about to clock off for the shift, having been in this hospital for far too long that day.

She traveled in the elevator down to the intensive care ward. The ethics committee's decision had left her reeling and depressed. She hated the fact that the policewoman's life had been adjudicated on the basis of its cost. And that no one, not even her ex, Peter, believed what she had seen.

The door *dinged* loudly as the doors slid open, and Naomi stepped out. Walking over to the nurses station, she was quite surprised that there was no one there to man it. Being a high-risk ward, there should always be at least one nurse on duty, at the desk, at all times, in case of monitor alarms.

Shrugging it off, she turned and walked in the direction of room 307. As she turned the corner to the next corridor, she slowed down. Not only was the corridor ahead shrouded in darkness, with the overhead lights having been switched off, but someone was emerging from one of the rooms. Teresa's room.

For a moment, he was nothing more than a shadow, a looming figure stepping across the dim corridor. The faint glow from the remaining lights barely outlined his form. Tall, broad, and dressed in a police uniform. His presence seemed strangely ominous as he walked in the other direction and vanished around a corner.

Feeling something was horribly amiss, Naomi quickened her pace and did not even glance in Teresa's room as she rushed ahead.

Turning the corner, she pushed open the fire exit door and entered. Staring over the railings, she peered up and down. As she fell silent for a second, she could hear the man's footsteps coming from below. Slow and heavy. She made sure that she trod as lightly as she could as she kept peering over the banister to see who this man was. But he remained constantly out of sight and always a flight ahead. No matter how quickly she moved, she never caught a clear glimpse of him.

She passed the first floor and continued down, making no sounds that might alert the man to her presence. The stairwell had also grown darker with each step she took as the faint lights above barely reached this far down to the lower levels.

It was only when she reached the bottom as she stood at the entrance to the grimy, old boiler room that she wondered what the hell she was doing. So what if someone went into Teresa Mallory's room? What difference did it make if a policeman came to see her? Why did she even chase this person down here? Just as she was shaking off her thoughts, rubbing her eyes, realizing how exhausted she had to have been and how silly this pursuit really was, a jet of steam hissed from unseen pipes, making her jump.

"Doctor Fowler?" a voice asked as a thin figure stepped out from the shadows. It was one of the hospital Janitors, Ed Martineau. Next to the leaking boiler, he stood, confused. "What are you doing down here? No one ever comes down here."

"I . . . I was following a policeman," she said, unsure.

"Down here?" Ed replied. "No one's down here except us two as well as a hell of a lot of really leaky pipes."

"Sorry, I must have been mistaken," she said with a nod and smile, stepping backward. "Have a good night."

Getting back to the ward, Naomi felt foolish and confused. She would not go back up to intensive care. She would just go home and sleep.

. . .

Across from the east side of the Queen of Mercy Hospital, a row of run-down tenements stood. The lights from the hospital wards shone out twenty-four seven, sending light across the surrounding neighborhood, burning like a weak sun that never dimmed among the dark night.

In one of the shabby apartments as the hospital glow broke through the edges of the thin curtains, Rafael DeGrazia held a large butcher knife up to his wife Sofia.

Grabbing a china display plate from the bookshelf, Sofia hurled it at her husband viciously. It smashed into pieces as it crashed into the wall beside him.

"Come on, then!" she screamed. "Do it, puto! You haven't got the cojones."

"Vete a la mierda!" he shouted at her, waving the knife angrily.

A sudden banging on the wall stole Rafael momentarily from his threat. A neighbor could be heard shouting. "Shut the fuck up in there. We're trying to sleep! I've called the police."

Sofia was not distracted by this threat but just turned to Rafael with a sneer of hate. "Go on. Cut me. They'll just catch you and cage you up like an animal."

As he shook his head, Rafael's thoughts were spinning. His eyes quickly filled with tears. "You fucked that guy," he said, distraught. "In our house!"

"No . . . He fucked *me* . . . right in the ass. On your side of the bed."

Rafael let out a furious scream and charged at her with his knife raised high. But before he could get close, the front door exploded inward with a crash. The wood ripped from its hinges as shards shot across the apartment like shrapnel.

In the cracked doorway stood a towering policeman. Matthew Cordell. His silhouette imposing against the dim corridor light above him.

Sofia, still reeling from shock, felt the tension in her chest loosen as a faint feeling of relief found its way into her.

Rafael, still in a blind fury from the betrayal, turned his knife to the policeman. He was over emotional and not thinking straight. "Fuck off! This shit is between me and my wife!"

But Cordell did not leave. He just stepped in, not drawing his gun, then took a swipe to grab the knife from Rafael's hand. But his stained-gloved hand missed.

The reality of the situation was setting in with Rafael as his fury began to turn to fear. "I just wanted to scare her. Here, take it!" he threw the knife onto the tabletop next to him.

"I wanna press charges against this asshole," Sofia said with a sense of victory.

Rafael stared at her in shock.

Both were so caught up in their own argument that they did not see the details of Cordell. They did not see the face or the condition of the uniform. But at that moment, Sofia got hit by the smell that drifted from him. The foul odor that made her wrinkle her nose in disgust.

Cordell, meanwhile, had picked up the knife from the table and held it up.

Rafael then caught sight of the policeman's face in the light as his bulging eye stared at the blade, then up to him. Before he could scream, Rafael could only stand in witness as the Maniac Cop's arm shot to one side, throwing the butcher's knife out.

It shot from his gloved grip and split the air, coming into a thudding stop as it embedded in Sofia's chest. Cutting her heart immediately in two. The impact sent her crashing backward into the kitchen, landing against the sink, knocking over piles of pots and pans onto the cold floor, before she fell forward.

Before Rafael could scream, before he could even make sense of what was happening, the Maniac Cop was gone.

Running over to his wife, Rafael could not stop the flood of tears. He could not find the words to speak. He gasped for air as he knelt beside her convulsing body. He tried to hold her in his arms as a torrent of blood shot out from her mouth and all over the floor. He wailed in horror as he grabbed her tightly, kissing her on the forehead. Desperate as if it could help her stay alive, he grabbed at the knife to remove it. But the blade tip had been caught tightly in her spinal vertebrae.

Sofia was long dead as the knife finally relented, and he managed to pull it out of her.

Then a gasp from the doorway stole his attention.

"What have you done?" a male voice asked. It was a neighbor who was standing in the doorway, horrified at the sight.

Dressed in a bathrobe, he had been woken by the commotion and had just enough of both Rafael and his wife's continual disregard toward others in the building. As his warning to them that the police had been called did nothing, he had decided to get out of bed and tell them in person what he thought of them. But he stared, aghast, at his neighbor, unable to think of a word he could say as Rafael gripped the murder weapon, held his dead wife, and blubbed.

"It wasn't me!" Rafael cried in desperation. "Didn't you see? It was the cop!"

But the neighbor had heard the screams from this apartment before. The shouts, the crashes, the sounds of chaos often spilled from the DeGrazias' apartment. So, as Rafael spoke, the neighbor didn't believe a word of it.

Rafael clutched his wife's body, his chest heaving with uncontrollable sobs. "I gave him the knife," he whispered. His voice was barely audible. "I'm so sorry." His own words echoed in his head, each syllable tightening around his throat like a noose, stopping the words from coming out. He knew how this looked. He knew what everyone would think.

Then came the wail of sirens from down the street, getting nearer by the second.

More gasps rippled through the hallway as more neighbors appeared and saw what had happened. Their eyes were filled with shock, revulsion, and fear.

Before the police could even reach the stairs, the shame, the grief, the weight of it all became too much. Rafael could not live with this. He could not live with the blame. He could not live without *her*.

With a final, whimpered breath, he lifted the knife and, without hesitation, dragged it down the inside of his forearms, slicing his flesh apart.

Chapter 5

As the sun dawned over the hospital, the morning shift staff started to arrive. Their footsteps echoed down the sterile corridors as, one by one, the closed departments began to open. The machines were powered on, monitors flickering to life, and the smell of freshly brewed coffee mingled with antiseptic cleaners as a janitor mopped the floors.

At the reception desks, the duty nurses flipped through the overnight logs, stifling a yawn as they pressed play on the answering machines. Series of messages crackled through the speakers; routine appointments, frantic late-night inquiries, as well as the occasional wrong number.

Down the corridors, the sound of carts rolling signaled the arrival of orderlies bringing bland breakfasts to the patients. Lights blinked on in empty rooms, bed sheets changed, charts were checked. The hospital, which had partially slept, was soon fully awake, bracing itself for another day of the unpredictable, the urgent, and the inevitable.

In the neurology department, a young radiation therapist walked with an oversized cup of coffee in their hand. Having voiced morning pleasantries to the nurse in passing, the therapist sipped from the cup. A fog of exhaustion had followed her from her bed, and she really needed to focus by the time the first patient came in. You can't play around with radiation, after all. A slight mistake could result in—

As soon as she had pushed open the double doors to the X-ray room, the strong acrid stench of burning flesh hit her, just as the terrible sight of Kenneth Powers caused her to drop her cup of coffee to the floor.

There, on the table, the hospital director had been burned and irradiated to such a degree that all of his skin that the X-ray had touched had slipped off, showing the blackened bone below, cracked and brittle. Both of his eyes had long since burst, and the brains and flesh on the skull had been liquefied and dripped out of every hole.

A half an hour earlier, down in the laundry room, an orderly's yell had alerted the guards. Nurse Edith

Beechum's crumpled body had been found, having been cast down the laundry chute.

Stan Moonjean was assigned to investigate the deaths at Queen of Mercy Hospital, and he was far from pleased about it. He had already spent more than enough time there visiting Teresa and had no desire to linger any longer than absolutely necessary—especially not in a place teeming with germs, sickness, and the stench of antiseptic barely masking decay.

His mind was on the Maniac Cop, not this. Chasing that lunatic was his priority, not wasting time in a hospital on what he assumed were just unfortunate deaths. He hadn't yet seen the connections that would make this case his problem.

Before, when the Maniac Cop had been targeting mostly White victims, he was never put on the case. Now, though—now there were bodies dropping in this part of town. And whether he liked it or not, he was here.

"Doctor Fowler?" Moonjean called as he stepped into the prison ward. Naomi was seated by one of the beds, carefully rebandaging the wrists of their latest injured inmate, Rafael DeGrazia. "Can I have a word?"

Rafael had barely stopped crying but was otherwise quiet and docile. He just looked downward and did not meet anyone's eye contact. Lost in what happened to him.

Naomi turned as she put the finishing touches on the bandage, then stood. "Can I help you?"

Moonjean quietly raised his badge but did not speak. He did not want to rile any anger from the other patients. The ones who may have something to say to a Black cop.

"You've heard about the murders, I assume?" he asked in a quiet tone.

Naomi nodded, though it all seemed totally unbelievable to her. When the call came that morning, she was informed that many staff members had already refused to come into work. They were too shaken and too afraid. Yet Naomi had arrived earlier than she was supposed to and had been met with wide-eyed stares from others, especially as she knew both victims. But giving into fear? That wasn't something she carried with her. Besides, the prison ward was the safest place in the building.

"None of it seems real," she said, motioning him to the door. "Do you think that they are definitely murders?"

"I doubt either could have been an accident." Moonjean nodded. "We're just trying to figure out any possible connection between the victims that could have resulted in their deaths."

"Are you going to ask about my patients? If they could have done it?" She opened the door to the corridor and led Moonjean through. Across into her small office.

"Yes, I am, ma'am," he replied, quickly taking an offered seat as she sat behind her desk. "May seem like a too-obvious call, but I have to check every possibility."

"Officer—"

"Detective."

"Detective, this is a secure facility. There is no easy way out of here, and even if someone did manage to slip out, we have a full head count. Why would they kill, then come back?"

Moonjean smiled, appreciating the logic. The same conclusion he had come to. But as he said, he had to check. He then changed tack. "I heard you and Nurse Beechum were friends?"

Naomi shook her head. "Not really friends. Work acquaintances."

"And you had a run-in with Mr. Powers recently?"

"A run-in?" Naomi replied incredulously. "Hardly. I had an argument with him about a female patient, a police officer. I was appealing for his committee to change their minds from turning off her life support. It was work, not personal and definitely not a run in."

"Police officer? Do you mean Teresa Mallory?"

Naomi nodded before remembering the uniformed man she had seen in the shadows, leaving Teresa's room. "Can I ask, did the department assign a uniformed officer to guard her?"

Moonjean looked at her, confused, he did not have to reply in words, Naomi could easily tell what the answer was.

"Well, there was one hanging around her room in the ward last night. I followed him down the stairs, but I lost him in the basement. So, if you're looking for a lead, well, Teresa Mallory is a link between the Powers and Edith. She looked after Teresa, and he was about to have her support turned off."

Moonjean thought for a moment with his best poker face. Things were falling into place. He was starting to see the bigger picture. "If you don't mind me asking, why did you follow the cop? Was he acting suspiciously?"

"I don't know, there was something about him. But I couldn't really see, as the lights were off. He was huge, though."

"He scared you, but you followed him? Down into a basement?"

Naomi shrugged. "I've got no idea why, but I was told that she had been put in here by a man in a uniform. That maniac cop guy."

Moonjean didn't say a thing. *Could this really be his work?* he thought. He was suddenly very glad he did not refuse to take on the investigation, which he was very close to doing. *Maybe it was fate that he was here now?* He had to make sure he remained logical in all of this.

"Or maybe it was just an officer there for someone else. On the job?"

"I've got no idea. I just saw this huge guy, followed him foolishly, then lost him."

After a few more minutes of polite questions, Moonjean said his goodbyes, then continued the investigation around the hospital. As he walked away from the prison ward, his mind churned over what she had just told him. A uniformed officer with no official assignment? Teresa being a link between the victims? And, of course, the whispered name that sent his mind spinning, the Maniac Cop.

He needed to dig deeper. If Teresa Mallory was somehow central to all this, then maybe she wasn't just another comatose patient—maybe someone or something, was making sure she never woke up. Could he be dealing with revenge?

He had to stick to the facts. No matter what his gut told him, he couldn't afford to sound like a lunatic by crying wolf over a man risen from the grave, even if he knew for a fact that such a subject was not from the pages of a horror book.

The day went by fast, where the hospital went about its ususal business, even with its skeleton staff. The murdered bodies were removed, the rooms sterilized, and patient appointments resumed. It was something the hospital was more than used to doing. Removing the dead and resetting everything, having to act like nothing had happened and carrying on to try and save the next patient through the doors with total focus. Death never slowed them down. And the patients had no idea what had happened.

By nighttime, there was very little activity on the surrounding streets. Only a few homeless people wandered around to stay warm, some straggling dealers sitting on corners waiting for the desperate to come out of the woodwork.

On one of the side streets, a young prostitute waited for any business. The chill of the night made her wish she didn't wear a leather miniskirt. Having had only one customer that night, she was keeping warm with the chain smoking of cigarettes. She just wanted one more john before she called it a night. She had bills to pay and didn't want her apartment's heating or water to be cut off again.

Her eyes widened in delight as she saw a late-model Ford slowly pulling up. Behind the wheel, a man smiled at her. Silently asking for her to come over.

She threw her cigarette down onto the sidewalk, then approached with the most seductive smile she could muster.

She had been a striking beauty once, fresh-faced, wide-eyed, but the streets had a way of carving years into someone fast. Though only twenty-one, the hard nights and rough life had aged her beyond her years. Her once-smooth skin bore the subtle lines of exhaustion and the blotchiness caused from her daytime addictions.

"Hello?" the man inside said hesitantly, playing innocent like so many had before him. His voice had a nervous edge, the kind that either meant he was new to this or just bad at pretending. "I-I was just visiting someone at the hospital . . . Thought maybe I could use a little cheering up."

She smirked, already knowing how this dance would go. They all had a story. A wife who didn't understand them. A rough day at work. Some excuse to justify them being here. She didn't care as long as the money was good.

One whispered negotiation later, drowned out by the wail of a passing ambulance, she opened the driver's side door and slid inside, flashing him an easy smile.

The car didn't need to go far. Just a quick reverse down a nearby alley, tucked in between two brick buildings, where the streetlights barely reached. The moment the car came to a stop, his hands were immediately on her thighs, eager and hungry.

She climbed onto his lap, straddling him as the warmth of their bodies and deep exhales quickly fogged up the windows. A slow, deliberate grind against his lap made him exhale, his hands gripping her hips as she rolled them against him. Her lips hovered near his ear, teasing, her breath hot against his skin.

"Relax, baby," she purred, digging her nails into his shoulders. "I have exactly what you need."

She reached down and unzipped his trousers, rubbing inside.

In the dim, steamy cocoon of the car, the moment blurred into something that, for a fleeting moment, almost felt like passion but was only transactional.

As had happened multiple times across this city in the past few days, they were rudely interrupted as the driver's side car door was opened from outside.

With only his uniform able to be seen, the policeman outside rapped his billy club on the car's roof, indicating he wanted the occupants of the car to get out.

"Aw, shit!" the driver exclaimed in a moan, desperate to finish off what he was doing but also desperate to get home.

She, though, smiled as she got off his lap. "Don't worry, honey, I'll handle it." Sliding off him, she got out of the car and readjusted her clothes, pulling her panties back up.

The driver did not wait for her to speak as he quickly undid his seat belt, zipped up his trousers, and lost his erection fast. "Hey, my wife's in the hospital having another kid," he callously explained as he went to step out. "I don't want any trouble, Officer. There must be some arrangement we can come to?"

At once, the policeman slammed the car door shut, narrowly missing the driver's face, stopping him from exiting the car. He then pointed to the driver to leave.

With a smile, the driver nodded. "Thank you, Officer!" he said through the closed window. Without waiting another moment, he turned on the car's ignition, stepped on the gas, and drove away. Leaving the woman standing there in the mouth of the alley to face the huge cop, who was now spinning his billy club over in his hand. Back and forth, it spun to be caught again as it turned then spun back again. The sound of the wood hitting his gloved hand reverberated loudly around them.

The girl was dwarfed by his presence, and as she stared at his face in the half light, she saw his horrific features and also noticed the old tattered uniform, covered in mold spores, burns, and filth. And that smell . . . She had no idea about the Maniac Cop. She had only arrived on the bus from Boise after that had all happened. She also would never have heard the name Matthew Cordell. She just thought it was an old gross cop who had not cleaned up.

She knew better than to react to anyone's grotesque appearance. She had been with even grosser people in her line of work. And as she knew all too well, you should be wary of the good-looking ones, not the ugly. So, she just averted her eyes and spoke with her practiced happy tone. "You must be new around here. They call me Lucky."

Cordell did not respond. He did, though, stop spinning his billy club and just stared at her.

She continued. "I always take care of you cops, and you guys take care of me. Know what I mean?" She dreaded what she was about to do, but she saw no other way. This man was hideous. His stink was enough to make anyone gag, but she had more important things to do. She had to avoid arrest at any cost. *Any.*

She slowly sank down on her knees as a big fake smile crossed her face. "I'll do all the work. I don't mind. You can just stand there." She reached out, but instead of going straight for the crotch, she reached out and took hold of the tip of his billy club. Drawing it closer toward her, she fondled it suggestively, caressing it as if it were *that* part of his body.

Her hand ran up and down the club, which he held firmly in his grasp . . . . threateningly. But to her, it was no threat. She could not see the danger here. She just saw what she had to do.

As her hands stroked the wood, she then moved her hand down the shaft as if masturbating it.

"Do you want me to?" she asked suggestively.

As she did, she quickly felt part of the billy club move. As her hand fondled it, the body started to come loose. Her motion had unscrewed the top half, and it slid off in her hand. She stared in surprise as this sheath came off, revealing the long stiletto blade within.

Her suggestive look and playful smile immediately dropped.

Another passing ambulance masked her terrified scream that followed. The shadows of the alley hid the violence as the Maniac Cop thrust the blade repeatedly through the face of Lucky, whose luck had just run out.

As Matthew Cordell wiped the blood from his blade onto his trouser leg, he pried the billy club's sheath from the dead prostitute's grasp.

He had no idea what he was doing. No control. No choices. From the moment he clawed his way out of the dirt, he had been running on instinct. Acting, not thinking. Staring down at Lucky's lifeless body, he felt nothing.

The last time he had held any real control was when he exacted his vengeance on those who wronged him. But even then, there were moments when his actions weren't his own. He killed because he had to. No thought. No plan. Just murder.

And he couldn't leave. Whenever he tried to step beyond the city's blinding lights, he found himself right back where he started—at the gates of Queen of Mercy Hospital. He didn't question it. He couldn't. Thought had no place in what he was. The hospital and the streets surrounding it were his entire world, the only ground he could walk, even if he didn't understand why.

Once, his mind had been consumed by the memory of his execution at Sing Sing, replaying in an endless loop. Since then, there was only emptiness.

He stepped out of the alley, leaving Lucky's body behind. A new pull gripped him, an invisible force tugging him back toward the hospital. The fourth floor. That was where he needed to be.

Sliding his billy club away, he reached for his pistol, checking the chamber. Six bullets. That would be enough.

An hour later, within the prison ward of the Queen of Mercy, most of the patient prisoners were fast asleep. Some tossed and turned, loudly moaning from their nightmares. Something that was commonplace in all jails and prisons. Most inmates, injured or not, from any walk of life, were regularly plagued with night terrors and scary dreams. More so than other folks would be.

Frank Jessup, in his curtained cubicle, lay on his bed. His bullet wound on his chest was raw, despite healing, and ached even with the pain medication.

He was asleep and, like the others, was having disturbing dreams that made his face twitch.

He did not wake as a dirty, white-gloved hand placed the loaded handgun on his pillow.

It was not until twenty minutes later when he rolled over in his bed that Jessup felt the hard metal press against his forehead, and he woke with a start. His eyes blinked open as he stared at the gun.

He looked around. The curtain surrounding his bed was still.

He listened. Everything in the ward was quiet.

Not believing what was happening, he checked the barrel and, like Cordell had done, saw it was fully loaded. His cuffed hands restricted his movements, and he smiled as he slid the weapon under his pillow.

Across the ward, Rafael DeGrazia was asleep on his back and, unlike the others, was having a dreamless night. He did not wake to see the large shadow of the man who murdered his wife cross over him. Nor did he feel the surgical probe that was slid into his cuffed hand. A long, hooked pick-like instrument that, while made to explore wounds and cavities, was a dangerous weapon in the hands of the violent or desperate.

In the far section of the ward, Kenyon had woken up from his dream and soon noticed that a key had been placed in his handcuff lock. Ready to turn and release the shackles. He then saw that on his bedside cabinet an open straight razor had been placed. Glistening in the moonlight that came in through the window.

Unlike the others, he immediately wanted to move. He undid the cuffs from his hands and his only leg. He then seized the blade between his teeth, then slid out from under his covers, down to the tiled floor.

With murderous intent, he crawled along the tiles, across the shadows of the ward, over to the door. Peering out of the small window, he saw an intern nurse speaking with a police guard. Both looked confused as they motioned to the unlocked and open security doors in front of them.

Turning back to the ward, Kenyon knew he needed help. Having one leg would do nothing against a group of guards. He then saw that Rafael DeGrazia was staring right at him from his bed, with the pointed probe in his cuffed hand.

Crawling back to his bed, Kenyon kept low, every movement slow and deliberate to not alert anyone. He grabbed the key from his unlocked handcuff, and with the straight razor remaining clenched between his teeth, he turned to crawl over to Rafael. His heart pounded in his chest, but it was not from fear but from murderous exhilaration.

Reaching DeGrazia's bed, Kenyon unlocked his cuffs.

Without a word, they exchanged glances. They were both armed. Both knew exactly what needed to be done if they had to escape. But they had different reasons. Kenyon, as he wanted to be free to live and Rafael, as he wanted to be free to finish the job and die. But not in a hospital.

"Check the other beds," Kenyon said, his voice barely above a whisper.

Rafael hesitated nervously, gripping the key tightly before nodding. He crept across the dimly lit ward, scanning the room for the other occupied beds. But there were only three of them in the ward. Looking beyond the curtain of the cubicle, he saw Jessup. He was lying motionless, his eyes closed.

Rafael slid to his bedside and gently shook his shoulder. "Hey. Wake up."

Jessup's eyelids snapped open. He was about to pull the gun out and fire until he saw Rafael hovering over him, dressed in the same hospital gowns as he was.

Rafael quickly unlocked his cuffs, but as Jessup tried to move, he grunted in pain, his chest wound making it impossible to stand on his own. His face contorted with frustration.

"Help me to that damn chair," Jessup rasped quietly as he nodded to the wheelchair beside his bed.

Rafael hooked an arm under Jessup's, then dragged him over to the wheelchair. Jessup wasn't walking out of here, but with a weapon in hand, he sure wasn't powerless either.

By the time they walked back across the ward, Kenyon was already on his foot, balancing on one leg, gripping the open straight razor.

"Who gave us these?" Rafael asked, motioning to his pick.

Rafael shrugged.

"Does it matter?" Jessup added. "We got 'em. We need to use 'em if we wanna get out of here and not get sent down. Right?"

"I'm innocent," Rafael replied sadly.

"Sure," Kenyon laughed under his breath. "We all are."

Jessup looked out of the room to the security doors, which had been closed, then at the policeman back at his station on guard.

Thirty minutes went by with nothing happening. At the guard station, the officer on duty was annoyed. He had come on shift to both sets of security doors being left wide open. The previous guard was nowhere to be seen. Who knew how long it had been open for? With the intern assuring that the patient headcount was all correct, they just locked the doors again and carried on, planning on not telling anyone.

When he could be bothered, the guard would check the CCTV to see when his colleague left, but he was too tired to do anything except sit there and read his magazine.

Just as he was getting into an article about hunting. The entrance buzzer sounded. Looking up to the monitor, he could see the ward nurse, Buddy, standing in the opposite corridor, wearing freshly washed scrubs, ready to start his shift.

Buddy took out his passkey, then scanned it. The first security door opened. He stepped inside. With his wide girth, this small space was uncomfortable for him to be in.

The guard pressed his button and released the second door. Buddy walked in with his usual smile. "Morning, boss man," he said.

A few yards down the corridor, the intern was gathering the patient reports for the doctor to look at when rounds started. He saw Buddy approach and smiled.

Before they could say hello, all hell broke loose.

The door to the ward flung open.

Kenyon bolted out, lunging with a furious roar at the guard, his straight razor raised then swiping forward.

Jessup sped out his wheelchair into the legs of the intern, sending them falling to the floor with a pained cry. Jessup then got his gun and aimed it at the intern's head, ready to fire.

Rafael had gripped the hooked probe tightly and held it at Buddy's throat. His bandaged arms slightly bloody from the wounds bleeding from beneath.

"Don't hurt me. Don't hurt me!" Buddy said in a high-pitched cry as the probe pressed against his neck. Despite his huge physique, he was useless. Too scared to try to fight.

Jessup, meanwhile, grabbed the intern and pulled him closer to the wheelchair. The gun's aim was not wavering.

The guard, meanwhile, was slumped in his chair, his throat cut wide open as blood gushed out in pulsing floods down his front and all over his magazine.

Jessup sneered at the intern. "What time does the woman doctor come on duty?"

"N-Not for a-another thirty or forty minutes."

"We can't wait that long," Kenyon complained, the straight razor still bloody in his hand as he grabbed the gun from the holster of the dead guard.

"Smash that camera," Jessup said, pointing up to the CCTV camera that peered down at them.

Rafael turned and grabbed a nearby stool.

Before Buddy could think to run, Kenyon stole his gaze with a murderous stare as he held up the razor. He simply shook his head in warning for the large nurse to not try anything, which Buddy complied with, being too terrified to do anything else.

As the stool smashed the camera, it cut off the security feed in the corridor. But at the same time, an alarm sounded loudly.

"Shit, let's get out of here," Jessup shouted.

His plan was thwarted. He wanted to stay and wait, to wait for Naomi. But the alarm forced his hand.

Kenyon looked over to the second ward of prison patients. Through the window, even in the dark, he could see the faces of others in their beds. All of whom had been awakened by the alarm sounding. None of them were given any weapons.

These were also lower security prisoners so with no need to be handcuffed to their beds.

One prisoner had hobbled out of bed, unhooked his IV bag, and carried it with him as he limped forward to the door. Another, suffering from severe burns, wrapped in thick bandages, followed.

At the far end of the corridor, in the solitary segregated room, Felicia watched all of it happening. As the only woman here, she clutched her book of fairy tales to her chest. She had no intention of escaping. She had nowhere to go.

Only two other prisoners made it to the hallway, and the rest decided to stay. Jessup looked at Kenyon, the two being the obvious ones in charge as they held the guns. "We can get out over the roof if we can make it up the stairs."

"Let me help you," Rafael offered as he walked behind the wheelchair to push Jessup along.

Kenyon, with a razor and a revolver, pressed the security door button as he motioned for Buddy to walk first and open the second door. Which he did, just as his bladder released in fear and stained the legs of his scrubs.

First through the doors and into the long corridor, Rafael pushed Jessup, whose gun was up and aimed straight ahead. He had all intention to kill those who tried to stop their escape. Behind them, the hostages, Buddy, and the intern, followed nervously. At the back were the two other prisoners that helped Kenyon along.

As they traversed the Renal Care ward, the group were soon spotted by a nurse who had heard the alarms and were on their way to investigate what the problem was.

Immediately, Jessup fired a volley of shots at her,

narrowly missing her head. She turned and fled in terror.

The shots were so loud they prompted screams and cries of concern from the patient rooms.

The convicts carried on toward their destination. The fire escape. Buddy and the intern held onto each other with fright, left with no option but to go with the escapees.

Around the corner, two orderlies wheeled a patient on a gurney. Seeming to have not noticed the gunshots or distant alarm from the prison ward. Seeing the armed prisoners approaching, they instantly bolted, leaving the patient on the gurney, alone and unprotected. A gurney that blocked the corridor to their escape.

The escapees quickly approached and, presuming no threat, pushed the gurney aside.

But as they passed, the man on the gurney moved.

He'd spun around to face them as they walked away, the sheet covering him fell off, exposing a gun in his hand.

It was Stan Moonjean. Having been nearby when the alarm sounded, he had rushed over and come up with the fastest plan he could. One that was, in retrospect, more foolish and dangerous than genius.

He took no pause in firing three shots at the back of the prisoners. Rafael and the two newer escapees were the first to fall as Moonjean's killshots ripped through their heads. Buddy and the intern dropped to the floor in terror, both in floods of tears.

Jumping off the metal gurney, Moonjean kicked it onto its side, putting a barrier between him and the last two prisoners. The ones with guns. Kenyon, with no person to prop against, held himself up with one arm against the wall. With his other, he fired his shots, each hitting the gurney with a thud. The bullets lodged in its surface.

Kenyon, thinking only of his own life, backed into a nearby room, frantically searching for another way to get out, hopping on one leg.

Jessup, meanwhile, had another method of escape in mind. He slumped down in his chair and immediately played dead.

As Kenyon hurried across the dark room, an elderly woman lay frozen in her bed, eyes wide with terror as he burst in uninvited. He barely made it halfway to the door when a gunshot cracked through the silence. The bullet hit him square in the throat, his momentum halting instantly before he crumpled to the floor.

The old woman's screams filled the room as Moonjean stepped in, gun raised, its barrel still smoking. He wasted no time hurrying to Kenyon's side and kneeling beside him. The man was choking, gurgling on his own blood, a gaping hole torn through his throat.

Kenyon was finished—incapacitated, beyond saving. Death was only moments away.

Moonjean snatched the gun from the man's grip,

wielding a weapon in each hand. Without hesitation, he turned to go, the old woman's screams trailing after him, their echoes lingering long after he was gone.

But as he stood in the corridor, something felt off. He glanced around, his gut tightening. Then he saw Buddy, still crouched, still terrified, wordlessly pointing behind him.

Moonjean turned. The fire escape door, which had been closed before, hung slightly open. And the prisoner in the wheelchair, Jessup, was gone.

He cursed under his breath. He'd fallen for it. Never even questioned the sight of the seemingly dead man slumped in the chair. He never thought the man would be playing possum. Seething, he turned toward the open door, his grip tightening on his gun.

Jessup was already halfway up the metal stairs, forcing his battered body onward despite the agony that tore through his chest with every movement. His barely healed wound burned, his breath ragged as he grunted loudly with each step, hauling himself upward, two steps at a time.

Reaching the rooftop access door, he shoved it open and stumbled out into the night. Smoke from nearby chimney vents swirled around, carried by the wind, turning the rooftop into a shifting, ghostly haze. He pressed forward, his balance growing worse, but he had no intention of going down quietly. If escape wasn't an option, he'd make damn sure someone else didn't survive the night either.

Below, Moonjean moved cautiously up the stairwell. The echoing slam of the access door above told him he was on the right track, but he wouldn't make the mistake of rushing in blind. With both pistols raised, he took each turn with deliberate precision, every sense of his was on high alert.

As the open rooftop door finally came into view, he steadied his breathing and braced himself. The thick smoke outside obscured his vision, twisting in the wind, making it impossible to see beyond the threshold. He took a single step out onto the rooftop, sweeping his gaze from left to right. Then . . .

A gunshot.

A sharp, searing pain tore through his calf.

Moonjean cried out as the bullet ripped into his leg, the force knocking him off balance. He hit the rooftop hard, gasping as the impact jarred his body. Instinct took over. He rolled toward the nearest wall, pressing his back against the cold brick, teeth clenched against the pain. His breath was loud but his grip on both guns remained tight.

Somewhere in the smoke, laughter echoed.

"You enjoy that?" Jessup taunted, his voice carrying through the smoke, reverberating and sounding as if it had come from all around Moonjean. "Guess we both have a handicap now."

Leaning against one of the smoking vents, Jessup grinned through his immense pain. The struggle of his escape had reopened his wound, blood seeping through the bandages soaking into his hospital gown. But he had no time to dwell on any of it. The cop was still alive. Still after him. If he wanted to make it out, he had to finish him.

He held his breath as he forced himself to move, slipping into the thickening smoke to the left of him. He used it as cover, circling back toward the access door along a long stretch of pipes. Each step he took was as deliberate and quiet as he could muster, despite the weakness in his limbs. His vision was blurred, and he felt sick, his pulse thundering in his ears, but he pressed on.

Then . . . movement.

A shadow.

A flicker of fabric against the access wall.

Jessup's grin widened. Without hesitation, he fired twice at it. Expecting to hear the thud of bullets on flesh and the screams of the cop.

But bullets ripped only through material.

There was no cry of pain that followed.

He moved closer through the smoke. As the target came into view, realization struck too late. Moonjean's jacket was hanging from the wall. A decoy.

"Freeze, or I'll shoot," the voice rang out behind him.

Jessup's grin faltered. He stood motionless, with his back to Moonjean.

"Drop the gun and turn around. Hands above your head."

"Say," Jessup mused as his grin returned. "How about a deal? I turn around and fire at you . . . Right between the eyes . . . and you? You try to stop me? Sounds fair?"

"I said drop your damn weapon and turn around," Moonjean snapped. He stood his ground, blood soaking his leg, balancing all his weight on his good one. "You're under arrest. Anything you say—"

"Blah, blah, blah," Jessup scoffed. "Come on, let's make it interesting. I mean . . . I might not even have any bullets left. Should we find out?"

Then he moved.

He spun, gun rising—

Moonjean fired both of his guns at once . . . and both bullets hit home.

Jessup's fingers slackened around his weapon without a chance to pull the trigger. He glanced down at the two new wounds in his chest, just above the one that was already there. His lips parted slightly. Then, to Moonjean's surprise, he smiled. Not a smirk. Not malice. Just . . . peace.

"Thank you," Jessup murmured.

The gun slipped from his grasp, clattering onto the rooftop. His knees buckled.

"How the hell did they get those weapons?" Naomi asked in shock as she wrapped a fresh bandage around Moonjean's leg wound. His trousers were bunched around his ankles as he sat on the examination table, wincing slightly but staying still.

He was lucky the bullet didn't enter the leg and just gouged past it.

"I was gonna ask you that," Moonjean replied, shifting slightly. "The only ones they got inside were the guard's gun and that ice-pick-looking thing. But that doesn't explain how a police-issue revolver got in there or a damn straight razor?"

Naomi's brow furrowed. "Someone must have given it to them. Someone with access to a secure ward."

"You think it's that same cop you saw, too?"

She shrugged. "Well, a doctor doesn't normally have a gun to hand out, and the guard on duty is dead. Is there another likely suspect?"

Moonjean exhaled sharply. "Maybe that's the answer, then. You saw that cop outside Teresa's room, and now a cop's gun shows up in a secure ward? And right after two people were murdered here? It's all gotta be connected. That's the most logical conclusion."

He hesitated before adding what his gut was screaming at him, that this all tied back to the Maniac Cop. And that the Maniac Cop was a zombie. He wasn't ready to say it out loud. Not yet and not to a doctor. She would have him locked up for that suggestion.

"What's the prognosis anyway? You gotta take my leg?"

Naomi smirked. "You're lucky. It'll be sore, but as long as you don't overdo it, you'll be fine."

Moonjean let out a short laugh. "Don't overdo it? Yeah, that's likely."

For a moment, as she finished off dressing his wound, the room was silent, just the faint hum of hospital equipment filling the space.

Then, an uneasy feeling settled over Moonjean. A creeping dread, like something had been overlooked.

"When did you last check on Teresa?"

Chapter 6

Dr. Nathaniel Quinlan sat stiffly in the office of Kenneth Powers, feeling woefully unprepared for the chaos that had landed in his lap. As Powers's emergency replacement, he had barely begun to grasp the overwhelming number of problems that faced the Queen of Mercy Hospital.

Standing in front of him were Dr. Peter Myerson and Dr. Gilliam, the head of Neurology. Both men looked tense. They had demanded an urgent meeting with him and Quinlan could tell by their demeanor that whatever they had to say wasn't going to make his day any easier.

"You said this couldn't wait?" Quinlan asked, rubbing his temple, not hiding his stress or mental exhaustion.

"Did you read the report we emailed you about

Teresa Mallory?" Myerson asked. "The one about her brain waves returning?"

Quinlan hesitated. He hadn't had time to even drink his morning coffee, let alone read reports. But he wasn't about to admit that.

"I did," he lied smoothly. "So, what's the issue?"

Gilliam spoke up. "As you saw in the report, after nearly two years of persistent electrocerebral inactivity, essentially a flatline, we are now seeing a measurable resurgence of brain activity. That's a complete shift from her previous condition. It raises serious questions about what's happening to her."

"Okay . . . and?" Quinlan prompted, still not seeing why this required such urgency.

Myerson took over. "While I was checking on her, I noticed swelling in her lower abdomen. At first, I thought it might be internal bleeding, so I did a full examination and workup. And—" He handed a manilla folder to Quinlan. "I thought you should see the results for yourself."

Quinlan took the folder and opened it. Reading the first page, his expression sank almost instantly. The charts and test results there took him only a second to process, but the implications hit him like a brick. "How long did you say she's been here?" he asked, his eyes still locked on the paper.

"Nearly two years," Myerson replied gravely.

Quinlan shut the folder, exhaling sharply with a loud sigh.

"Sweet lord . . . We can't let this get out. Not until we find the person responsible." He looked up at each of them. "Who had access?"

Myerson shook his head. "It isn't a secure ward . . . So, anyone. But before she died, Nurse Beechum mentioned something . . . She said an orderly from the prison ward had been down here, taking photos of the patient. He'd be my first suspect."

Buddy's hulking frame nearly filled the narrow locker room as he lumbered inside. The events of the previous night stuck with him like a fever dream. Having been taken hostage and the feeling of utter cowardice and helplessness. Even now, he still felt that same fear.

Human Resources had told him to take some time off. They suggested counseling, a way to process everything he went through. But Buddy didn't want that. He just wanted to be here, back in his routine, where things made sense.

Reaching his locker, he spun the combination dial, clicking through the numbers before the door creaked open. As it did, he peered inside, and a slow smile spread across his face.

Glancing around to make sure no one was watching, he pulled the scrubs from their hanger, revealing the hidden contents behind them.

Rows of Polaroids lined the walls of the locker, meticulously arranged. Naomi had seen a few of them, the ones he had let her see. Harmless, sentimental snapshots, or so she had thought. If only she knew the truth.

The rest of the pictures told a far different story. Some of his *models* had been alive when he took the photos. Some were from the morgue. But most were posed in ways that left no doubt they hadn't had a choice in the matter.

Still grinning, Buddy began to undress, preparing to slip into his scrubs. But before he did, he stood there, naked, staring at his images. His lips moved in whispered prayer, muttering to God and the angels.

But his hands weren't clasped together in devotion. They were grasping something else something large, flaccid, and unresponsive.

He wasn't praying for the patients in the pictures.

He was praying for himself.

He began tugging hard but with no effect as he grimaced and prayed.

Lost in his ritual, he didn't hear the quiet footsteps coming up from behind him. He didn't sense the presence of another, a figure even larger than he was, getting closer.

He only realized he wasn't alone when something cold and solid pressed against his shoulder, a billy club.

Before he could react, it looped around his throat and tightened.

Buddy's body jerked in surprise, his massive hands flying to his neck, clawing at the weapon that dug into his windpipe. A strangled gasp escaped but the grip on his neck didn't loosen. Buddy's size, his strength, didn't matter anymore.

The man behind him, Cordell, was bigger. Stronger. And he had the advantage.

Buddy thrashed, his feet slamming against the cold metal lockers, his vision swimming as his lungs screamed for air. But there was none to take in.

The pressure increased.

His face turned blue.

Then . . . his body went limp.

Cordell moved quickly. He yanked the nearby fire hose from its mount, unspooled a long length, then wrapped it tightly around Buddy's neck. With barely any effort, he hoisted the unconscious orderly up and dragged him toward the window as if he weighed nothing.

The window outside the fourth-floor locker room opened wide into the evening sky, allowing the cold wind to rush in.

With a single, effortless motion, Buddy's massive bulk was hurled through the opening. His body tumbled forward, deadweight in a free fall, plunging toward the pavement below, until the fire hose snapped taut and a sickening *crack* rang out.

His body lurched violently as his neck twisted, the sudden force nearly tearing his head from his shoulders. The thick cord bit deep into his flesh, breaking the skin, causing blood to immediately pour down his naked torso. Painting it red.

And there, he hung—lifeless, swaying in the breeze. His vacant eyes stared out blankly, his blue face locked in a grotesque scream for air.

Back in the locker room, everything remained untouched. The metal door to his locker stood slightly ajar. And inside, tacked neatly among the others, was the Polaroid that had sealed Buddy's fate.

The newest addition to his collection.

Taken in the dead of night.

One Naomi wasn't shown.

Teresa Mallory.

Naked.

Posed for his pleasure.

Naomi Fowler sat, curled up on her couch, dressed in her pajamas, the dim glow of a single lamp casting long shadows across the small living room of her Queens apartment. The telephone was pressed against her ear, her fingers gripping it tightly as she listened to Moonjean's voice on the other end. Her eyes were shut, struggling to process what he was telling her, biting back the nausea rising in her throat.

"It can't be Buddy," she said, her voice barely above a whisper.

Moonjean's heavy sigh came loudly through the

phone. "They found pictures of Teresa. Along with over fifty other women. All naked. Posed. Some of them . . ." He hesitated as if searching for the least horrifying way to say it. "Some of them, he . . . put things in. For the photos." His voice came through the receiver, thick with disgust. "That was him. Not that cop you saw. Seems I jumped to conclusions. Maybe that cop was Buddy in disguise. You said he was a huge guy you saw."

Naomi swallowed hard, gripping the phone tighter. "He may have taken the photos. He may have done those horrible things," she said slowly, forcing herself to think past the horror. "He didn't kill all those people. Or plant the gun? No way. But mostly, he's definitely *not* the father."

A long silence. Then Moonjean, cautious. "What makes you say that?"

Naomi hesitated as she spoke. "Because Buddy . . . Buddy couldn't father a child. He couldn't. I know that because he came to me once. He had an . . . issue. Some kind of accident when he was younger. He wasn't . . . able to get an erection. Or even ejaculate."

"And you're sure?"

"I wouldn't say it if I wasn't. He came to me for help. I ran tests. A *lot* of tests. Not sure I should have, but I felt bad for him."

Another long pause.

Then Moonjean muttered, more to himself than to her, "Then, that means Teresa's baby belonged to someone else. And if he didn't do anything as you said, then someone could be using Buddy's sick obsession as a cover."

"Moonjean," she whispered down the phone. "If Buddy wasn't the worst of it . . . then it's gotta be that cop, right?"

Silence on the other end. Too long.

Then, finally, Moonjean spoke.

"There's something else. Some medical equipment went missing in the last couple of days. Burglary division is looking into it, but does this mean anything to you? Could it be linked? At this point, I feel like everything is connected in that hospital. There's too much happening too quickly."

Naomi frowned. "What kind of equipment?"

"Resuscitators, mechanical ventilators, an EEG machine. All gone from the hospital's equipment store."

Her heart pounded. "How? How the hell does someone get into the prison ward and arm the inmates without showing up on CCTV, then walk out with an entire load of equipment from a secured storage room that's guarded twenty-four seven?"

Moonjean's voice became muffled for a moment, distracted by something on his end. She could hear someone speaking to him, though she couldn't make out the words. Then he came back.

"Listen, you mind if I come by to talk about this in person? I just gotta handle something first."

Naomi hesitated.

"Sorry to drag you into this more," he added, sensing her uncertainty. "But with everything happening at the hospital, speaking to someone who actually understands and knows the place . . . it helps."

She sighed. "Uh . . . sure. I guess. It's 221 Temple Street, off Queens Boulevard."

As Naomi hung up the phone, she let out a long breath.

She stood from the couch, moving toward the kitchen without bothering to turn on the light. Her feet followed the same familiar path as she pulled open the refrigerator, bathing herself in its cool blue glow. She reached for the milk carton, but her mind was elsewhere.

She regretted agreeing to let Moonjean come over. He was relying on her too much. As if he didn't trust his own instincts. He had to be breaking a dozen regulations just telling her half the things he had said.

Maybe he liked her? He was a good-looking guy.

But . . . no. Not now. Not after everything that had happened.

A fresh wave of sadness stung her chest . . . Buddy. Nurse Beechum. Kenneth Powers. Even the inmates. How could any of them—

A moldy, white-gloved hand shot out of the dark and clamped over her mouth. She could feel that through the material were fingers, clammy and cold.

They crushed against her nose, silencing her before she could scream.

The milk carton slipped from her grasp, crashing to the floor, white liquid splattering across the floor.

She was yanked backward, dragged through the kitchen, through the door, and into the night.

Forty minutes later, Detective Moonjean pulled into the driveway of her house in his unmarked vehicle, the engine growling before he turned it off.

Stepping out, he barely had to take two steps before he saw it.

Her front door was wide open.

His gut cried at him that something was wrong.

"Dammit," he muttered, already pulling his gun from the holster.

He limped forward as fast as his injured leg would allow.

Fearing the worst, he stepped inside.

Teresa Mallory lay motionless, her chest rising and falling in forced rhythm with the respirator. The noise of the machines filled the dim hospital room, her EEG monitor flickering wildly with bursts of activity. Her eyelids fluttered, rapid eye movements beneath them showing the depth of her dreams.

Beside her, Dr. Sylvester, a general practitioner

brought in for consultation, methodically checked her vitals. Heart rate. Blood pressure. Reflexes. All were stronger than he would have expected. With an ultrasound scanner in hand, he smeared lubricant across her abdomen.

Standing across from him, Dr. Peter Myerson and Dr. Quinlan observed in tense silence.

"I don't feel right about any of this," Peter murmured, his unease clear. "We almost turned off her life support a few days ago. And now this?"

Quinlan exhaled sharply, his expression unreadable. "We have to be sure, and if we are, we have to correct it."

"But how the hell was she brain-dead for nearly two years, and now she's—" He gestured at the monitors. "Could these machines be reading the fetus instead?"

Quinlan said nothing. He didn't have an answer. None of this made sense.

Dr. Sylvester finished his scan, turning to the others with an expression of surprise. "Well," he said, "her blood pressure and heart rate are stronger than some of my more active patients. And the baby?" He glanced at the monitor. "Developing well. There's nothing physically preventing her from carrying it to full term. Which I believe she should. After all, it's not the child's fault—"

Quinlan's jaw tightened. "Full term?" His voice was filled with annoyance. "That would be *obscene*."

Sylvester arched his brow but said nothing.

Quinlan shook his head. "You were brought in as a third party to determine if she could survive surgery. Not to advocate for her rapist's fetus."

Naomi Fowler's eyes fluttered open, and immediately, she was met with the sharp, pulsing agony of a migraine. The intensity was blinding, a familiar pain she hadn't experienced since childhood, back when the crushing stress of a violent home life had made them a frequent affliction in her life. She had thought she had outgrown all of that. Left the pain behind. But one had returned with a vengeance.

A cold solid pressure pressed against her back. The floor. Marble. Cracked and worn. Turning her head slightly, she could see that she was sprawled on the ground, still in her pajamas.

Then, as she tried to move, the cold bite of metal against her wrists caused her to yelp in alarm.

She was handcuffed.

Her arms were pulled tightly across her chest, the cuff's long chain locked her to a rusted steam pipe that ran up the wall beside her.

Gritting her teeth against the pounding in her skull, she forced herself to take slow, deliberate breaths. She was alive. That much was clear. But where?

Painfully, she took in her surroundings. Even the dim light here stung her.

She could see that she was inside a church. Or at least what had once been one.

The moonlight through high shattered windows cast the cavernous nave in a ghostly silver hue. The rest of the room was caked in shadow.

The pews had been removed from their usual place in front of the altar and stacked haphazardly in the far corner. Their use reduced to little more than discarded wood.

She didn't know it, but she was back near the Queen of Mercy Hospital. Only a few hundred yards from its main entrance.

Then her gaze fell on the other side of the room. To the makeshift hospital bed that had been set up. Beside it, the missing medical equipment from the hospital sat. The resuscitator, the mechanical ventilators, the tangled tubes to be attached to a patient.

And draped across the bed was an NYPD officer's uniform.

Teresa's uniform.

She had no way of knowing for sure yet, but Naomi could feel that she was not in immediate danger.

She had been taken for a reason.

She was here to serve a purpose.

To tend to the needs of the patient who was still to arrive.

.   .   .

Teresa Mallory was wheeled into the surgical theater, her body motionless beneath the white hospital sheets. The rhythmic hum and beep of the life support machines followed her, their tubes and wires trailing behind as lifelines. Though she lay utterly still, her presence was undeniable, and she was not gone.

The procedure she was to have was routine. The outcome was predetermined. They were going to remove the baby.

Inside the theater, the surgical staff moved with quiet efficiency. Surfaces were wiped down, sterile gloves snapped into place, and the instruments were arranged in perfect order.

Outside, the hallway was silent. No voices. No movement. Just the lull of an empty hospital corridor.

Inside, the surgical team took their positions as Quinlan entered, his pace was brisk, his purpose focused. He nodded toward the attending physician, signaling him to proceed.

Then the door swung open again.

Dr. Peter Myerson stepped inside.

Quinlan barely was able to conceal his irritation. "This is routine. I don't need you here."

"I'm sorry, sir, but I have to insist," Myerson implored. "This pregnancy is the reason for her sudden brain activity. If you terminate it, she'll most likely relapse into a vegetative state."

Quinlan turned away from him. "Then, write a

paper about it," he dismissed coldly. He turned to the surgeon. "Proceed."

Peter stepped forward. "But—"

"Leave, Doctor."

The weight of the order left no room for argument. Myerson held his tongue, forced back his anger, then turned and exited, the door swinging shut behind him.

Quinlan exhaled slowly, then returned his attention to the procedure. His mind was elsewhere. Every decision he had made up to this point had been to bring this disastrous situation to an end. The pregnancy, in his mind, was the last piece to clean up before normality could return.

He saw none of the connections.

The prison ward breakout? Separate issue.

Buddy's "suicide"? As far as Quinlan was concerned, it was a confession to what happened here.

Kenneth Powers and Nurse Beechum's murders? He had already decided an orderly must have done that, too, eliminating them to cover up his crimes against Teresa. The police had seemed to agree.

In Quinlan's mind, this was the last step. The final problem to be erased.

The attending physician took his scalpel, poised for the first incision.

Then . . .

A collective gasp from the surgical team.

Teresa's eyes were open. Pale blue, unfocused, staring blankly upward.

"Oh my god," someone whispered. "She's awake."

The lights cut out.

Instant, total darkness.

The machines also cut out. Their rhythmic beeps ceased immediately.

Then the doors crashed open as something moved through the darkness like a shark.

A wet, sickening rip.

Dr. Sylvester barely had time to gasp before a powerful hand seized him by the throat, then tore his larynx out in one brutal motion.

A nurse screamed but was instantly silenced as she was hurled across the room, crashing into the rest of the surgical team, sending them sprawling in a mess of limbs and shrieks.

Then came the sound of heavy boots against the tiled floor.

One by one, those boots found them.

Crushing. Stomping.

Each impact brought an abrupt *crack* and another death.

Quinlan reacted fast, snatching a scalpel from the tray. He turned, heart pounding, blade raised.

Then the figure turned to him.

Quinlan lunged, driving the scalpel deep into the massive form's chest.

The blade sank in with ease.

It made no difference.

There was no falter. No hesitation.

The figure reached for him.

Quinlan did not have time to inhale as his head was wrenched clean from his shoulders.

His body collapsed to the floor, blood arching in the air around his lifeless form.

Then . . . silence.

The hospital had been teeming with police officers. After the wave of violence that had torn through the Queen of Mercy over the past week, the building had become more of a crime scene than a medical facility. Yellow tape sectioned off key areas, evidence bags piled up, and officers moved through the halls taking statements, documenting, trying to piece together the chaos. Though the official investigation had begun to get to the same conclusion as Quinlan, that it may have been the work of one deranged orderly, they still investigated to tie up all the loose ends.

And not one of those officers in the building heard the massacre that happened in the operating room. A massacre which would destroy all their theories.

No one saw Matthew Cordell as he carried Teresa Mallory's limp body through the hospital's unseen paths, slipping through the cracks they had failed to guard.

They had the front covered. The back. Both wings.

They had officers in the parking lot.

But they had no one below.

Beneath the Queen of Mercy, a stairwell ran down the west side of the main building. It led from the fourth floor, past Pathology, Pediatrics, and the intensive care ward, finally descending into the sub-basement levels.

Naomi had followed the large uniformed figure down here once. But she hadn't gone far enough through.

Because beyond the rusted old boiler lay an opening. A tunnel.

Years ago, overhead lights had once illuminated that path but those bulbs had long since shattered, leaving only dead sockets and the hanging remnants of their cords.

It was pitch black down there, but Matthew Cordell didn't need to see to walk through it.

He strode with certainty, Teresa draped across his arms like a rag doll, limp and unaware.

The tunnel stretched for several hundred yards, then, at the far end, another cracked opening.

Cordell stepped through.

Instead of another basement or another hospital wing, he emerged into the overgrown brush outside the perimeter of the hospital.

The wild, untended vegetation swallowed the tunnel's exit, masking it completely, even under the sunlight that sometimes shone down on it. It was a forgotten place.

Cordell pushed past these weeds and vines, and

the foliage fell back into place as though sealing the path behind him once again.

He climbed the embankment to the road. And there, in the distance, the Queen of Mercy was a storm of chaos.

The discovery of the operating room had only just happened. Sending officers into a frenzy. This attack was the worst. The one no one could dismiss as an accident, which some officers had tried to do with the past deaths, not totally convinced of Buddy's guilt. In the case of Nurse Beechum, some posited that she could have fallen by accident down the chute. In the case of Kenneth Powers, some thought it could be a simple yet horrific suicide. But . . . this latest set of murders . . . it was, in no doubt, what it was. That is if they could find the bodies. They only found the blood. The vast amount of blood.

Police swarmed the hospital, their movements frantic and confused as they scrambled to make sense of the scene.

They scoured the wards.

They searched the wings.

They sealed the exits.

Still cuffed to the steam pipe and laying on the cold, cracked marble floor of the church, Naomi could hear the sirens of police cars in the distance. For a moment, she believed that help was coming, that they knew where she was, but when they screamed by and headed to the hospital, she sank into more fear. This feeling only grew when she started to hear the heavy footsteps walking from the rectory at the back of the nave.

Through the dim shadows, Cordell soon lumbered out, carrying the body of Teresa over to the makeshift bed next to all the stolen hospital equipment. Laying her on it carefully.

The large rotten figure then turned to Naomi. Staring at her for a few uncomfortable terrifying moments. The light from one of the high broken windows illuminated his grotesque face, his missing nose, his one bulbous and one withered eye, the mass of large, dried open gashes that covered his flesh.

"What the hell happened here?" Moonjean asked as he stood at the door to the wreckage in the surgical theater. The room itself was smashed to pieces. No machine or item had been left untouched. Blood coated each wall thickly. Dark, gloopy arterial spray having horrifically redecorated each surface.

But they had still not found the bodies. No physical remains of the surgical staff, the operating physician, or Doctor Nathaniel Quinlan. Their DNA was coating the whole theater, but no flesh or bone.

An officer stood next to Moonjean, looking just as

surprised. "No one knows. Three surgical staff, two doctors, and the patient . . . just gone."

Moonjean sighed. "Well, I don't think all this blood's from one person, so I think we're looking for corpses."

He knew Teresa was the missing patient and, because of that, could only presume this was the work of Matthew Cordell. But why? And How did he know where to find her?

In the church, Cordell stood intimidatingly close to Naomi as she reconnected Teresa to the stolen hospital monitors. Face mask, tubes, and wires reattached, the respirator switched on. Electrodes attached from the EEG machine. All were soon on and beeping, hissing and humming away as Teresa was once as she had been, straddling life and death in the vacant space between. The machines helped her to exist, though were not the only thing keeping her alive.

NYPD officers combed every corridor, every stairwell, every room. Their flashlights cut through the dim, sterile hallways of Queen of Mercy Hospital, illuminating patches of darkness as they moved, trying not to incite panic among the remaining patients and staff.

They found nothing. No bodies. No signs of a struggle beyond the surgical theater.

The operating room, drenched in gore, was the only evidence that anything had happened at all. There were no blood trails leading away, no signs of movement beyond those initial moments of slaughter. Outside those doors, it was as if the massacre had simply ended, vanishing into thin air.

Still, the officers scoured the building, frustration mounting with every empty hallway. The sheer brutality of the scene demanded an answer, but their only viable suspect, Buddy, was already dead.

Theories spread like wildfire between the officers who moved in pairs. Some whispered that there had to be more escaped prisoners from the ward. Others were convinced it was the work of a serial killer. Some even suggested a mass suicide orchestrated by a cult.

But only one man suspected the truth. Detective Lieutenant Stanley Moonjean.

He knew.

Even if he couldn't prove it yet, he felt it.

And then the call came in. His walkie-talkie crackled to life, cutting through the tense silence.

"Moonjean, we need you in the morgue. We found 'em."

The morgue was colder and more impersonal than the rest of the hospital. With walls lined with rows of body drawers and a room of empty metal slabs. It was not a nice place to visit.

Moonjean arrived to find an officer standing stiffly beside a morgue attendant, both looking pale and shaken.

He didn't need to ask if it was bad news. He could see it in their faces.

The attendant, an intern who looked like he had seen too much too soon, swallowed hard and stepped toward the wall of storage drawers.

"No bodies were brought in during the past twenty-four hours," he explained with a hollow voice. "And as of this morning, these drawers were empty."

Moonjean frowned. "And now?"

The attendant's hand hovered over the handle to one of the larger compartments meant for bulkier persons. "Now," he explained, "we found blood on the floor outside one."

There was a moment of hesitation. A second where the intern seemed to consider whether he really wanted to go through with this.

Then, with a low, metallic groan, he pulled the drawer open.

There they all were. Five bodies. Crammed into a space meant for one.

A grotesque tangle of limbs and contorted faces, pressed together in gory intimacy. Their bones had been shattered, their flesh torn and compressed as they had been packed into this tight space. Even their clothing, soaked through with congealed blood, had fused together into a single mass of shredded fabric and ruined flesh.

At the forefront of the twisted heap was Nathaniel Quinlan. His mouth was locked open, his wide eyes frozen in a terror that had not left him in death. The others were so tightly packed against him that it was impossible to tell where one ended and the next began.

Moonjean had seen horror before.

Murder. Mutilation. The worst of what human beings were capable of. But this—this was something else.

He forced himself to swallow back the bile rising in his throat. A rare reaction for him.

The officer beside him wasn't so lucky. Turning abruptly, he staggered toward a nearby trash can and heaved, vomiting noisily into it.

The morgue attendant, perhaps the most experienced of them all, kept his eyes averted, refusing to let the image burn itself into his memory. But he knew it was already too late.

Moonjean took a shaky breath and turned away. He needed to focus.

The killer came down here.

Then where?

He looked at the attendant. "Is there an even lower level than this?"

The man nodded, his voice barely above a whisper. "Yeah. Subbasement levels. The boiler rooms. But it's not accessible to the public."

Moonjean exhaled sharply, already reaching for his walkie-talkie. "This is Detective Lieutenant Moonjean. Sergeant Oakley, are you there? Come in."

A crackle. Then a voice.

"Go for Oakley. What do you got, Moonjean?"

He glanced once more at the grotesque pile of bodies before turning away. "I need to know—has anyone cleared the subbasement yet?"

A pause.

A long pause.

Static hummed from the radio.

"Stand by."

Something in Moonjean's gut told him that's where Cordell went.

"As I told the officers I showed down here an hour ago, these are the old boilers from before the central heating system was put in," Ed Martineau, the janitor, explained to Moonjean as he led him down the stairs to the subbasement, both holding flashlights. Moonjean limped, but he was in not much pain, not enough to slow him down.

"Nobody comes down here much anymore," Martineau continued. "It's just the cleaning store, so only me and my team ever come down."

As they reached the bottom of the stairs, the dim orange lightbulbs on the ceiling cast an orange glow over the room, making the grime and decay all that more apparent. The dirty walls, rusted pipes, and puddles of brown liquid that dripped onto the uneven floor all glistened under the pale light. Along one side of the room, newer metal shelves had been set up. They held row after row of cleaning supplies. Bottles of liquid disinfectant, spare mops, brushes.

At the far end of the room, Moonjean swept his light across a brick-lined doorway.

"Where does that lead?"

Ed shrugged. "Dead end. The tunnels collapsed years ago. You can go a way in, then that's it. They used to be the maintenance tunnels below the old hospital. I'm talking way back, like in the twenties. But they fell in decades ago."

"How come?"

"Water damage, I think. Every time it rained, it seeped down through the dirt."

"Is that safe to have beneath a hospital?"

Ed let out a short laugh. "What are you, a building inspector or a cop?" But when Moonjean didn't share his amusement, his smile faded. "Look, I told the last cop, I haven't stepped in 'em for years. You wanna? Be my guest, but it's not safe in there."

The janitor's beeper suddenly chimed loudly. Grabbing it off his belt, he glanced at the display before muting the alarm. "Guess they're ready for the cleanup now. You okay down here on your own?"

"Sure."

"Well, watch your step." The janitor trudged back up the stairs, leaving Moonjean alone.

Leading with his flashlight, the detective walked farther into the room, past the rusted boilers and dust-covered pipes, toward the brick opening to the tunnels. As he stepped in, he felt the ground change from solid concrete to packed dirt.

Moving cautiously, he took each step slowly. His flashlight swept across the ceiling, the beam caught on the remains of the shattered lightbulbs. The walls, once solid brick and concrete, had begun to erode, revealing rough stone and patches of raw earth where water had seeped through.

The air down here was uncomfortable to breathe. It was heavy with a damp, thick stench. Moisture clung to everything down here.

He had ventured about a hundred feet into the passage when a thought crept in that maybe it was time to turn back. It felt unstable here. The walls seemed fragile as if barely holding themselves together.

But as he thought this, his flashlight caught the dead end ahead.

Nodding to himself, he resigned—

Wait . . . What is that?

Something was ahead, caught in the flashlight beam. Something dark to the right of the collapsed end.

He focused the light and walked forward with caution. The collapse had left heaps of rubble scattered across the dirt floor as the walls buckled inward. But there, beside it, was a massive opening. The edges of this hole were too clean, too deliberate. It wasn't water damage that caused this.

Something had forced its way through here.

As he got closer, he could also tell the hole looked fresh. And it wasn't just wide enough for a normal man.

It was wide enough for something much larger.

Something like Cordell.

Stepping over the rocks at his feet, Moonjean stared into the breach, into the void ahead of him that seemed darker than the tunnel he had come down. The air beyond felt colder and drier.

"Not a dead end, then," he murmured.

He pulled his gun from its holster apprehensively.

"You can do this," he whispered to himself, stepping through the jagged opening.

His flashlight shone through the darkness on the other side, but there wasn't much to see. Another tunnel, but this one had no water damage. The walls were brick-lined. It had to be an entirely separate tunnel that had been broken into the hospital's damaged ones.

He moved forward, gun steady, slightly limping.

After fifty yards or more, the tunnel ended and opened up into a larger space—a vast, shadow-filled chamber.

Moonjean hesitated before entering, letting his light look first. Along one of the walls lay forgotten fragments of religious artifacts. Wooden crates leaned haphazardly against the brick, their contents half-spilled onto the floor. Dozens of old candleholders and dust-coated hymnals that hadn't been touched in years.

Further along, Moonjean gasped as he nearly fired a shot. The light had caught on a collection of figures. But as his heartbeat steadied, he exhaled. Just statues. Life-sized saints stood in various poses, their features eroded by time and neglect. Some were missing noses, arms, or entire sections of their forms.

As he stepped in, he realized that this must be under the church across the street from the hospital.

Had he really walked that far? He could have sworn he'd only gone a short distance, but somehow, he had passed beneath the parking lot, under the road and ended up here.

His light finally settled on a set of wide wooden stairs that led upward.

Moonjean slowed his pace as he took the first step. The wood creaked beneath him, the sound reverberating around the chamber. Another step. Another creak. His arrival would be no secret to anyone listening.

He moved as softly as possible, climbing carefully, his flashlight angled downward to keep the steps in view.

After two dozen cautious steps, he got to the top and paused.

Pressing his back against the doorframe, he slowly stepped into what he could see was the church's nave.

Quickly, he switched off his flashlight so as to not catch any unwanted attention. The moonlight streaming through the high windows provided just enough for him to see.

He looked around at the vast space before him. Piles of rotting pews sat abandoned to one side.

Then he heard it.

A soft, rhythmic *beep . . . beep . . . beep*.

His gaze locked onto the hospital bed in front of the altar. Tubes and wires leading to the machinery surrounding it. The blinking lights flickered in sync with the beeps, casting tiny pulses of illumination across the room. A cluster of oxygen tanks stood upright nearby, their dull metallic surfaces reflecting what little light reached them.

As he moved closer, he saw her.

Teresa Mallory. Lying in the hospital bed. But this time, she was dressed in her crisp New York Police Department uniform.

Sidling up to her bed, he looked at her face. The perfectly pressed uniform. The steady rise and fall of her chest. The soft whir of the respirator accompanying the rhythm of her breaths.

He was close enough to touch her—

When something in the shadows to his left reached out and grabbed *him*.

Chapter 7

As the hand grabbed his arm, Moonjean shuddered and lashed out with the butt of his pistol, narrowly missing Naomi as she managed to duck out of the way.

"It's me," she whispered in a panic.

Quickly, he lowered his arm as he realized who it was. He saw her pajamas, the cuff around her left ankle that traced to the nearby wall, keeping her prisoner. She was shivering from the cold and looked petrified yet determined.

"Thank God you came," she said, keeping her voice quiet. "I thought it was him."

"Is it Cordell?" he asked.

Naomi nodded. "I saw his badge. He wears it on his uniform . . . Look, we don't have much time." She motioned to her manacles. "Can you help me out of this?"

"I don't have any keys," he said as he then looked at

his gun. "Right . . . turn away. As soon as I shoot, if he's around, we gotta get out quick, okay?"

"Where is everyone else?" she asked, sounding helpless.

Moonjean shrugged with an apologetic smile. He didn't have to explain to her how he came on his own, it was now obvious. "We just gotta run, okay? We can call in backup when I get you safe."

"What about her?" Naomi said, looking at Teresa.

"We gotta unplug her," he explained. "She wouldn't want this. Not that baby. Not being taken by him."

"She won't last long," Naomi said. "He brought her here unplugged, and she was nearly gone then. I had to resuscitate her. She won't last even a few minutes off that thing now. It'll be murder."

Moonjean turned and looked sadly at Teresa, at the woman he remembered. "I knew her. You didn't. And you weren't there to see what he did to her."

"What if she can come back from this?" Naomi asked. "It's medically possible. Especially with all we have seen."

"If she woke up, it would be a nightmare."

He turned to her bed and grabbed the tubes from her body, yanking them off forcefully.

Naomi wanted to stop him but knew that, despite her protests, he was right. Who would want to give birth to that child . . . if it even was a child?

Taking her respirator mask off, the only thing left

on her were the electrodes that monitored her brain and the beeps of her heartbeat.

Within a few seconds, the brain activity monitor was flatlining as was her heart. As if she had been waiting for him to do this, she finally gave up the fight, and the *beep-beep, beep-beep, beep-beep* turned into one continuous tone.

Not wanting to waste any more time, Moonjean walked around to the long stretch of chain shackling Naomi to the wall and fired his gun at it. The bullet cracked through one of the links. The sound deafeningly echoed around them.

Naomi did not react to it as she stared at one of the monitors. The heart rate monitor. It emitted a continuous flatline tone. But the line on the machine wasn't flat, not entirely. There were small, almost imperceptible rivets along that line, too weak to force a change in the tone. Rivets that appeared in a rhythm.

Moonjean, though, heard something coming from outside. "Is that a police siren?"

Officer Asher Phillips had gotten out of the academy and joined the ranks of the NYPD six months prior, and from day one, he had felt like quitting.

From a long familial line of officers, Asher was the youngest. His three older brothers, his father, grandfather and great-grandfather, even his mother, were all on the force.

He had grown up listening to the stories—the heroic tales from all members of his family doing their duty and saving the day. Something Asher saw in his future.

But since joining, he had been relegated to the sidelines at almost every turn, and he knew why. His mother.

She had friends throughout the higher ranks of the force, and he had heard from fellow officers how she had called in favors to keep him out of danger. So, when any big call came in, he was given something as awful as traffic control.

As his colleagues were stuck in the thick of the action, Asher was far away, and they never let him hear the end of it. Of course, his mother denied such intervention, but here he was again, down the road from the Queen of Mercy Hospital, where a killer was on the loose.

Parked on a decrepit street, his and his partner's job was a simple one, keep the lookie-loos away.

But they were in a dead-end part of town. The lookie-loos here would be armed or high as a kite and not listen to a cop asking them to leave.

His partner, though, loved their assignments.

Officer James Davies had gone his whole nineteen-year career actively avoiding danger as well as avoiding diets. He was a short man whose width was almost comparable to his height, and all he wanted was to ride out the years, collect the paycheck, and go home to his wife and dog. Nothing else.

He had never even withdrawn his weapon from its holster while on duty, something he was proud of and something Asher would never understand.

Sitting in their patrol car, they turned on the siren again to keep their presence known—something they were to do every five minutes for an hour. One down, eleven sirens to go.

James laughed as he noticed Asher's hangdog expression.

"Aw, cheer up. At least you're not getting your asshole pulled out of your mouth by some psycho."

"We could be catching him right now!" Asher moaned. "But instead, we're stuck here, corralling the assholes away from the action."

"Well, would you rather this or be killed in action?"

Asher grimaced instead of answering as he opened the door to the car and got out. "I'm gonna have a smoke."

"See?" James said after him. "You couldn't do that if you were over there. They get no breaks."

Lighting up his cigarette, Asher leaned on the car bonnet as he took a long drag. The only concession to being out on the vacant streets. It may have taken months, but it was right here, and now that he finally decided he would hand in his notice to the NYPD, his family would hate it, but he could not carry on like this.

As he dwelled in his morose thoughts, he began to think of what his life could hold next. What his—

"Hey, over here!" a voice shouted from one of the buildings, stopping Asher's train of thought.

James heard it, too, and turned to look out of the driver's side window. He immediately saw where the voice had come from—the once-boarded-up window of the church. He also recognized the person sticking his head out to get their attention.

"Moonjean?" James said to himself quizzically as he got out of the car. "What the hell are you doing in there?"

Asher walked around and looked at his partner. "Thought that place was boarded up."

"Hey," Moonjean shouted. "Patch through to headquarters. Get SWAT units into position around the church. You two cover the front of the building until they arrive!"

"What?" James replied loudly, confused. "Aren't you supposed to be at the hospital?"

"There's access through a tunnel in the subbasement."

James as always, was hesitant. "Okay and?"

"This is where that maniac cop's been hiding out. Now, fucking call it in!" Moonjean then disappeared from view.

"Maniac Cop? What the hell is he talking about?" James grimaced, not wanting to be in the middle of anything, especially about that.

Asher was the polar opposite.

"Aw, fuck yeah!" he exclaimed, barely able to contain his excitement. "I'll call it in!"

Climbing down from the broken window, Moonjean felt some semblance of satisfaction. "With a little luck, some firepower will get here before Cordell gets back. Now, let's get out of here."

"You told me yourself that guns haven't stopped him before. What makes this any different?"

Moonjean didn't answer. He had noticed Naomi, who was still staring at the heart rate monitor.

"What are you looking at?"

"It's not possible," Naomi muttered as she moved over to the bed and placed her ear against Teresa's uniformed belly.

"She's dead," he said.

"Shhhh." She focused her attention, closing her eyes as she did.

Thump-thump, thump-thump, thump-thump. The tiniest of rhythms.

"I can hear its heartbeat," she said in shock as her eyes opened, and she stared at Moonjean.

"Can babies have heartbeats this early?"

She shook her head.

"She's dead . . . but the baby . . . it's . . . it's alive." She stared in horror at him. "How is this possible? How can a dead man father a baby?"

The sudden sound of gunfire could be heard from outside the church.

"Shit!" Moonjean cursed. "He's here." He turned to Naomi. "Keep behind me, okay?"

She didn't answer, she was too terrified.

"We stayed too long," he said nervously as he quickly drew and rechecked his revolver. "Shit!"

Outside, both Officer Asher Phillips and Officer James Davies wished that they had called in sick. But neither would call anything ever again.

The side door to the church, with its boarding ripped off, creaked as it opened. Moonjean and Naomi hurriedly retreated into the shadows of the alcove behind the altar.

Cordell had returned.

He was more shadow than man in the darkened nave. His immense figure loomed larger than ever as he stepped forward.

He had first come back with a mind full of revenge. He then came back a second time in a fog, hearing other voices in his head, pulling him in directions he had no desire to go. Now, he did not think at all.

His heavy steps echoed through the vast emptiness of the church as he approached the bed where Teresa lay, still dressed in her uniform. His pace soon slowed as he saw what had happened.

The life support system had been disconnected, its tubes torn away, leaving only her lifeless body lying before him.

Then a sound, low at first, swelled into a terrible, guttural moan. It erupted from deep within him, a cry of anguish without logic or language, only raw, primal grief.

It reverberated through the building like the mournful chords of an organ, filling the space with a sudden aching lament.

His mind may have been a void but his instinct told him one thing: he had lost his mate.

The agony of that realization twisted through his decayed, ruined body, making him seem less like a monster and more like a creature to be pitied, a thing trapped in torment, unable to do anything but wail in sudden sorrow and rage.

As his head dropped, his gaze falling to the floor, his cries turned to growls.

They only increased as he saw the broken chain that had held Naomi.

His gaze then shot up and around the room, trying to see where she was. The one who was to blame in his mind.

From outside, a cavalcade of sirens descended on the street. Police vehicles arrived in force, Officer Asher Phillips's last act as an officer coming to fruition.

Cordell heard this and paid it no attention. He was more focused on finding Naomi.

But Moonjean and Naomi had snuck out from the shadows and climbed up the spiral staircase leading to the choir loft.

They now took refuge behind the broken remains of the once-proud pipe organ, wedging themselves in a corner where they hoped they could not be readily found by Cordell.

SWAT had arrived. They saw the bodies of Officer Phillips and Davies. The limbs were torn off and piled in pieces on the bonnet of their squad car. Their guns lay on the floor, having only a chance to fire off half of their bullets.

"It's him, isn't it? It's the Maniac Cop. He's back?" one SWAT officer said, a look of terrible fear in his eyes.

He had witnessed the Maniac Cop's destruction before as had this whole squad. They were all there at that St. Patrick's day parade. They had seen the Goliath's carnage.

Their usual bullish confidence shrank as they all looked terrified to each other.

"You think Moonjean's still in there?" one asked.

"He's probably dead already."

"Well, we gotta do *something*."

"What about the tunnels that he talked about?"

"What can we do? *What the fuck can we do?*" another asked in a panic.

Matthew Cordell ascended the spiral staircase of the church, his footsteps slow but deliberate.

Moonjean and Naomi crouched in the shadows beside the pipe organ. Naomi, trembling, squeezed her eyes shut, praying for this all to pass. But Moonjean, he was somewhere else entirely. His body was here, but his mind was lost in the past.

As they fled up the stairs, desperate to escape, Moonjean had risked one last glance. And in that moment, he saw it, the monster's face, bathed in moonlight, twisted in agony, roaring with heartbreak. A face not of the living but of the dead, wrenched back to life by some force. A face of pure, undiluted rage.

Moonjean's theory was confirmed. Cordell was a dead man walking.

Raised in a culture where the deceased did not always stay buried, where zombies were not just Hollywood nightmares but woven into belief and heritage, he had suspected what Cordell was already. But as he gazed upon the grotesque certainty before him, there was no more room for doubt, and that filled him with a fear that almost crippled him. It's one thing to believe something unbelievable but a whole different beast to see it manifested in front of you.

Cordell was resurrected. And Moonjean knew that

with every fiber of his soul. He knew that Cordell was not just a brutal man on a mission of revenge but a force from the void of the dead. The Maniac Cop carried with him the same haunted look as something that now crippled him in fear.

Stan Moonjean was just a boy when he first saw the dead walk.

The jungle cemetery was a place of silence, thick with damp earth and decay. Graves that lay forgotten beneath creeping vines, with stones worn smooth by time. He had wandered too far that night, drawn here by a mix of fear and fascination, by the stories whispered among his friends.

And then, it stepped from the shadows. That thing.

At first, it looked like a man. But something was wrong. The way it moved, slow and deliberate, its body powered by something beyond death. Moonlight caught its face in the fading daylight, skin gray and lifeless, eyes like empty wells. Within it, no soul remained, only a hunger to destroy.

Moonjean couldn't breathe. His small body froze in place as the creature reached out for him.

The fingers, dry and cold, brushed his arm. A simple touch, yet it carried something foul as something almost seeped beneath his skin, into his bones. The boy opened his mouth to scream, and once it started, he couldn't stop.

And as he screamed and screamed, the monster screamed, too. The same primal roar of pain and anguish as Cordell wailed in the church.

When Moonjean's family found him, curled up and sobbing in the dirt, having run for his life, they did not ask what he had seen.

They already knew.

With Cordell a mere foot away from their hiding space and nowhere else to go, Moonjean grimaced as he grabbed the voodoo charm fetish he still wore under his shirt and pulled it out, displaying its protection front and center. He then pushed himself to his feet with a defiant scream, lifted his gun, and fired at the Maniac Cop.

Bullet after bullet, he fired all rounds from the chamber, dead shot into Cordell's head, sending the cop's eight-point hat spiraling off the balcony and down to the nave below, exposing his whole rotten head. The six shots had made clean holes in Cordell's pale and scarred skin, joining the many others. Without the hat, something that humanized him in a strange way, Cordell looked every part the monster he was.

The Maniac Cop, though, was barely stopped in his pace. As he reached out, grabbing for Moonjean's throat, his fingers instead got hold of the voodoo charm fetish.

For a second, Moonjean smiled. This would be—

Cordell cut the thought short as he ripped off the charm necklace and tossed it off the balcony beside him as if it meant nothing. It had no power over him.

Moonjean gasped. He was out of bullets and out of options.

Cordell seized the detective by the arm, yanked him closer, then picked him up off the ground. Within seconds, Moonjean followed his charm necklace tossed over the balcony, down eighteen feet to the broken marble floor below.

He plunged down, landing with a crunch on the tiles. The burly detective smashed into the floor with full impact, and as he did, his shoulder wrenched free from its socket, and his left arm snapped backward. His hip fractured and an agonized scream escaped his throat. The world above him spun, blurred by shock and pain.

And yet, through this haze, he could see Cordell coming back down the spiral steps, dragging Naomi behind him.

The Maniac Cop's grip was like stone, but he did not hurt Naomi. Not yet. Instead, he dragged her down the steps as she stumbled behind, screaming to be released. But resistance was pointless against him.

As they stepped out onto the marble, Cordell dragged her over to the hospital bed—to Teresa's motionless body.

He then released his grip on her, only to shove her

down beside the medical equipment. His message was clear. He didn't need words; he just pointed his finger at Teresa.

Naomi looked up at him, knowing exactly what he wanted.

Her heart pounded inside her as she shook her head. "I can't save her," she said with a tremble in her voice. "There's no way. I'm sorry. It can't be done." She looked up at him, desperate to try to get through. "Cordell? Matthew Cordell, right? You have to know this. You have to see that she is gone."

Cordell didn't react with words or anger, just cold, methodical movement.

He reached for one of the oxygen tanks stacked nearby.

One strike . . . that was all it would take. One crushing blow to shatter Naomi's skull like fragile glass. He lifted the tank up high, ready to bring it down over Naomi's head.

"Don't you think I wanted her to live?" she cried out.

Moonjean struggled to see. His entire body was consumed with pain. His vision blurred as tears welled from the sheer agony within him. Every movement he tried to make sent fresh waves of fire through his nerves.

Then . . . an explosion.

The deafening blast from the front of the church made him gasp. He wiped at his eyes, trying to clear his vision through the daze. When he finally managed to look, he saw it—smoke billowing from a new gaping hole in the church wall. The air rippled with the force of the detonation, dust, and debris cascading through the air.

And through this new breach, a volley of smoke grenades was hurtled in.

One of the metal canisters clanked against the marble and rolled to a stop just feet from Moonjean. A heartbeat later, it erupted, spewing thick, stinging gas into the air. He barely had time to react, rolling away with a pained cry, shielding his face with his uninjured arm.

Another explosion followed. Then another. More canisters tumbled through the shattered wall, filling the church with a suffocating cloud.

Cordell turned to this new intrusion and lowered the oxygen tank that he had been ready to crush Naomi with. He let it fall to the ground, landing with a hollow clang beside the other tanks.

As the smoke filled the room, with Cordell looking toward the new hole in the wall, Naomi scrambled backward, uncontrollably coughing from the unbreathable air. She got to her feet, reaching out blindly, searching for something solid to steady herself against. Her hand soon found the bed where Teresa's dead body lay.

And then . . . as the smoke became so thick that little could be seen, something gripped back.

For one terrible second, she thought it was Cordell. But it wasn't.

Smaller fingers wrapped around Naomi's arm. Her stomach turned to ice as she turned and saw the impossible.

Teresa was sitting up, grabbing at her. Her eyes were open, unblinking. The tear gas did not make her cough as it did Naomi. It did not sting her eyes as it should. Like Cordell, she simply existed, not breathing, not struggling. A body that was neither dead nor alive.

Her once-beautiful face, through the events of death, seemed more rigid, the flesh stretched tight over the bone. Her skin was graying. There was no warmth, no humanity in her.

Through the swirling smoke, Cordell turned.

He had been striding toward the hole in the wall. But something stopped the undead officer. His massive body shifted as hesitation rippled through him, his attention was stolen back by an instinct.

Then, he saw her. Teresa.

She stood, gripping onto a terrified Naomi, her police uniform the same one she had been meant to be buried in. Her posture, her presence—she was like him.

A fitting mate.

Cordell took a step toward her, then another, drawn by her.

She let go of Naomi and stepped toward him.

As they got close, his hand lifted, his fingers

brushing against the pale skin of her throat—the throat he had snapped in his fury long ago.

For a long moment, he simply stared. His head bowed slightly as though in remorse. A silent plea. Not that he had a memory of any of it.

Teresa's eyes, glassy and cold, looked up at him. With her hand, she lifted his chin.

There was no accusation. No hatred. No thought.

Another canister burst through the shattered window, tumbling toward the ground. But this time, it struck next to the cluster of oxygen tanks.

As the canister exploded, so did the tanks.

The result was immediate. A deafening, concussive blast ignited the highly flammable gas.

From that spot, the church erupted in fire, and Cordell and Teresa stood in the center of it, engulfed. Fire enveloped them, turning them into incandescent specters, figures wreathed in flames.

Through the blinding heat, Naomi forced herself around the furnace, coughing, choking, scrambling toward Moonjean on the other side.

Reaching him, she grabbed hold of his good arm and tried to pull him with her. But he barely had the strength to lift his head, and when he did, his broken arm and fractured hip debilitated him in pain.

Through the searing blaze, through the shifting smoke, Cordell and Teresa stood as one.

Finally, together.

But they did not stare at each other for long.

Now, they walked forward, through the heart of the fire, toward Moonjean and Naomi.

From the back of the church where Moonjean had first entered, a team of SWAT officers suddenly emerged, stepping into the smoke-choked remains of the church. Their rifles raised and fingers poised on triggers, they advanced through the destruction with trained efficiency.

Then they saw Cordell and Teresa.

Immediately opening fire, their bullets tore through the flame and smoke, hammering into the now advancing dead. But it was like firing into stone. Their rounds had no effect, just as they never had. Cordell and his resurrected mate were unfazed by the hail of bullets that should have torn them apart.

Naomi and Moonjean stood helpless in the debris, trapped between two forces. Moonjean used Naomi to prop himself up, the pain in his body making it almost impossible for him to stay upright. The SWAT team, ineffective to stop the Maniac Cop and his mate, at least managed to pull them to safety, helping them back to the tunnels, firing more rounds at Cordell and Teresa as they did.

But Cordell and Teresa ignored them all entirely. They had only one destination. Their uniforms on fire, their bodies charred, their faces blackened with soot and ash. They moved toward the broken hole in the front wall.

With the wind rushing in from outside, the fire had caught onto the few items in the church. The pile of broken pews at once side were now engulfed, and the remaining curtains that hung from the boarded-up lower windows were, too. Even the very boards that blocked out the light were now afire.

Outside, two figures soon emerged.

Cordell and Teresa, with the flames rising high off them, walked without fear toward the awaiting cordon of officers at the foot of the steps. For a moment, the police hesitated, not believing what they saw, even though some had seen the impossibility of Cordell before. But there was a female version of this impossibility as well.

They somehow expected Cordell to collapse. To burn as he did back at Sing Sing when he laid waste to his old prison block.

But both of the walking corpses kept on coming.

And then they attacked.

Cordell and Teresa tore into the first ranks of officers before any of them could react. Their burning hands gripped, tore, broke, smashed, and gored. Teresa was faster and stronger than she had ever been in life, lashing out with the same unrelenting force as Cordell, sending bodies flying, ripping them in two or crumpling to the ground.

When the gunfire erupted as ever, it did nothing.

Bullets tore through them, but they did not even pause. The flames that consumed them only seemed to act as an additional weapon as everyone they attacked also caught fire. Both of them were beyond pain.

The massacre was swift and horribly brutal. Blood, limbs, and gore flew as freely as the screams from the SWAT team's mouths. Their ranks disintegrated into chaos as the officers trampled over one another, desperately fleeing for their lives.

The SWAT commander tried his best to hold the line, just as he had outside the Rockefeller Hotel only a few years ago when he last witnessed the violence of this monster.

"Keep firing!" he bellowed, his voice rising above the carnage. "Keep goddamn firing!"

But his orders fell unheard. The noise around him was too great, his men abandoning him. As he turned to see where his men were, Teresa was suddenly upon him.

Her hands clamped around his body, lifting him from the ground. The heat from her charred, burning flesh soon caught onto his uniform, searing through his clothes, melting the very fabric into his skin. She did not crush him, did not tear at him. She just held him tight, fully aware that the fire sweeping over him was enough.

He struggled, gasped, and cried, but there was no escape for him.

And when his body sagged in her arms, she flung his still-burning corpse aside. His broken, burning body tumbled into a cluster of cowering officers. A discarded, ruined thing aflame, spreading its heat upon them with terrifying quickness.

Teresa didn't even look back. She just took a few steps forward and noticed something on the floor next to a fallen officer—a shotgun. She reached down, picked it up, then cocked it with one smooth motion.

The fire, though powerless to stop their advance, had still gnawed away at Cordell and Teresa, if only slightly.

Cordell's body was too much of a husk, his flesh long dried and scarred from past torment. His uniform, already singed and tattered, left little for the flames to consume. The fire simply clung to him, flickering uselessly, doing little more than illuminating his grotesque form.

Teresa, however, had more to burn. Though she resisted the flames longer than any living officer, her flesh was still fresh enough to suffer. The fire ate at her slowly, its hunger merciless. Her face, once beautiful, was half-destroyed, melted and ravaged. The once-soft features had warped beneath the heat, her skin blackened and peeled back in places, exposing raw sinew and bone beneath.

Her hair was gone, reduced to scorched remnants, the fire having stripped it from her skull.

But still, she stood.

Still, she moved.

Even in the tunnels, Moonjean, Naomi, and the remaining SWAT officers could hear the screams from the streets. A terrifying chorus of pain, the sounds of metal crunching, scattered gunshots echoing in the air. They could only imagine the horror they had escaped.

Within minutes, the battle outside was over. The police had been reduced to a gored and mutilated mass. Patrol cars lay freshly overturned, bodies scattered in the streets. The only surviving officers were the ones who managed to run away, too terrified to stand their ground.

The only movement came from those who were no longer living, Matthew Cordell and Teresa Mallory.

Ahead of them, the abandoned SWAT transport truck loomed.

Without a word, Teresa climbed into the back, slamming the doors shut. Cordell took the driver's seat.

The engine roared to life as the truck sped forward, smashing aside the police vehicles that blocked the road. Metal crashed, glass shattered, but nothing could stop it from driving off into the night.

Cordell and Teresa were loose.

Chapter 8

The buildings loomed on either side of Central Park, towering residential structures stretching into the sky, their windows glowing with light. From above, the park might have seemed peaceful, a dark oasis in the middle of the neon city. But down in the park, it was a different world. The tree line swayed gently by the tranquil lake as the moon skimmed across the water, giving the misleading impression that this was a serene and safe space. It was not. It was dark and dangerous, a place that, at this late hour, was not safe to walk alone.

A group of three junkie punks crouched in silence. Despite the park being known for its danger at night, people still thought it wise to cross through it. Businessmen late getting home. Families rushing to make a theater show. It didn't matter who. Anyone who crossed these punks would be fair game. They were waiting, prowling like a pack of feral dogs, eyes sharp, muscles tensed.

Then came the sound. The clack of heels on the concrete path. Approaching from a distance. Steady, unhurried. A woman alone.

The first punk, the leader, grinned with yellowed teeth from cigarettes and neglect. He whispered, "I'd say those are some sexy heels coming our way."

The clacking got nearer.

"Long strides . . . I bet them legs run all the way up to her asshole."

The leader then leered through the bushes to get a better look. From this distance, he could see from her silhouette that this woman was slender, moving with confidence and a long stride.

He could not help but let out a giggle of delight as she got nearer. "Wait till she is past us." He drooled, turning to his gang.

As she stepped by, all three punks quickly ran out of their hiding place to surprise her.

"Hey!" the leader shouted, making her stop in her tracks.

Then, slowly, too slowly, she turned to them. They were suddenly confronted with a sight that made them balk. A police uniform. A badge.

"Aw, shit, she's a cop," one punk moaned.

In the gap between the lights that lined the path, this section was caught in shadow. It was a place the punks had chosen to jump out for that very reason. They could be scarier in the dark. But here and now, it cast darkness over the policewoman.

"Didn't they give you a shitty beat to walk tonight?" the leader said, not dissuaded in the slightest as he rubbed his groin.

One of the other punks turned and leaned against a nearby tree, his hands raised, his legs behind him. A traditional pose for a suspect to take to be searched.

"What ya waiting for, Officer? Read me my rights," he joked.

Immediately, the female cop walked forward, past the leader and straight over to the punk against the tree. At that moment, the leader caught a glimpse of the cop's face. The burns. The singed remnants of hair. The look of murder.

Officer Teresa Mallory on her deadly beat.

The leader was too high. He had no way to react fast enough for this. He could only mutter, "What?"

The punk against the tree had been in scrapes with the law before. He'd been roughed up by the NYPD, shoved into squad cars, slammed against brick walls in dark alleys. He could take a punch, could handle the occasional cheap shot to the ribs. He expected some roughhousing as she got close. He expected her to try to dominate, but he would then turn on her. She was playing into his trap.

Then came the first hit.

A slap to his side. It should have been nothing. But the moment her hand struck him, a crack was heard. Agony exploded in his arm as the bone snapped clean through the skin. His body jolted as he screamed. But she wasn't done.

The second blow landed against his back.

Crack.

His vertebrae gave way like splintering wood, and a fresh scream followed. His legs buckled as he spluttered. But before he could fall, she grabbed him by the collar and spun him around. He had no time to register what was happening before her palm drove into his chest.

The impact sent a crunch through his rib cage, the bones snapping inward. The pain, indescribable and all-consuming, ripped through him as blood spewed out of his mouth, smothering his scream.

Through the blur of torment, he saw her terrifying face.

Her hand then went to search the last area. With a force that shattered his pelvis, her fingers dug through the jeans he wore, breaking through the fabric of his crotch and into his flesh. She took hold of what she could and tore it free.

The next sound was the sharp crack of a neck breaking, followed by the punk's gurgling cries cutting short.

The leader and the other punk had taken off, terrified by what they had witnessed. They sprinted down the winding path away from the murderous policewoman.

As they turned a blind corner, they skidded to a halt.

Ahead of them, blocking their path, was a huge shape. Matthew Cordell, billy club in hand, striding toward them.

"Shit!" the leader gasped, pulling his friend backward.

But they did not get away.

They ran straight back into the grasp of Teresa, who lunged forward, her bloody clenched fist still holding the other punk's torn-off genitals as it smashed through the second punk's face. Breaking his skull in on itself under her immense power. His eyes burst, his jaw cracked in half.

The leader screamed in terror as she turned on him, pulling her fist out and dropping the flesh in her hand to the ground.

"Please, no!" the leader punk screamed, backing away.

His foot caught on a small railing, and he fell backward with a yelp, tumbling into a flower bed.

With the wind knocked out of him, Teresa didn't relent. She stood over his gasping body and grabbed hold of the staked *No Picking the Flowers* sign that was in the earth next to him.

He could only scream as she raised the dirt-covered pointed end of the sign and slammed it back into his chest. The force broke through and out the back, embedding the sign back into the ground.

As Teresa turned and walked back onto the path, she gazed at Cordell, who stood close by, watching.

He was not participating. These were hers.

In one of the wards of the Queen of Mercy Hospital, Moonjean was all trussed up in a hospital bed. His shoulder and arm were in a cast, his midsection heavily bandaged. An IV fed him medication. He looked exhausted and in pain as he woke up.

Naomi, out of her pajamas and dressed in normal clothes and a white doctor's coat, adjusted his drip. She noticed him waking and smiled.

"Hi," she said. "Don't worry, you're at Queen of Mercy. I'm taking care of you."

"Why here?" he asked weakly. "They could come back. Kill us."

"We've got guards all over the place now. It's as safe as it can be."

"I gotta go, I gotta check in, we gotta catch him," he whimpered as he tried to move, but waves of fresh pain coursed through him.

"Hey, relax, okay? You're good to no one if you hurt yourself more."

A voice came from the doorway. "Doctor?"

Naomi turned and saw the police bodyguard.

He continued, "That visitor? He's still here."

She suddenly nodded, having forgotten they were waiting. She turned to Moonjean.

"There's a man waiting outside. He says he knows you . . . You okay if they come in? I have to go on my rounds anyway. Despite everything, I've still got patients who need me."

The night air had been cold over the past week, but a sickly humidity had suddenly settled over the city. The air hung, thick and unmoving, the lack of wind making it worse. Even open windows did little to offer relief.

In a Westside studio apartment, close to the Hudson River, the bedsheets clung to Charlie and Mae as they tried to lose themselves in each other. Charlie tried to make love to her, tried to fight through the discomfort of the humidity, but the noise outside shattered any rhythm he could find. The screams and crashes stole any passion from his loins.

Breaking away, he grimaced and slid out of bed, moving toward the window without a word.

"Where the hell are you going?" Mae groaned. "I'm not done yet!"

Charlie pulled back the shade, peering into the street, looking for the source of the noise.

"Get your ass back here," she said playfully.

But he didn't reply. He just stared down at one specific part outside.

"No fucking way," he mumbled.

Mae propped herself up on one elbow. "What is it? Junkies again?"

Charlie turned, his expression dark. "Stay away from the windows, okay?" His eyes quickly darted around the room. "Where's my camera?"

"Work?" She scoffed. "Now? Now you're thinking of work?"

But Charlie wasn't listening. He was already moving, tugging on a pair of jeans, stuffing his feet into his shoes without bothering to lace them. He yanked open the closet door, rifling through its contents until his hands closed around his camcorder. Flipping it open, he loaded a blank tape.

Mae sat up fully, the sheet slipping from her shoulders. "What are you doing?"

He turned to her with a glint in his eye. "*Criminals at Large.*"

"The TV show?"

"It'll make us a hundred thousand bucks," he smiled, already heading for the door.

"Not that maniac cop shit again?" Mae scrambled after him, grabbing his arm. "Remember last time? Or the time before? I ain't bailing you out again 'cause you get stuck in cops' business."

Charlie wrenched free. "You're with a gutter hack, babe. It's what we do. We chase this stuff down."

And then he was gone, disappearing down the stairs before she could say a word.

Charlie Coleman was a video journalist. The worst kind. He would throw his camera anywhere to get the shot. He had broken into crime scenes, houses, even sat in closets waiting to catch Z-list celebrities in an illicit encounter. And he had made quite a nice living from it. Nothing major, but his salacious work paid for his apartment and the food on the table. But he was also obsessed. Obsessed with getting footage of the Maniac Cop.

The reward from *Criminals at Large* had been mentioned many times by its presenter Donnie John, who still pushed the Maniac Cop angle as often as he could, trying to stir up new interest to get more viewers and content. He resurrected that story often as no single episode came close to the viewing figures about Matthew Cordell and Stephen Turkell.

But *Criminals at Large* got one thing wrong. It believed what they had been told, that Turkell was the Maniac Cop and Cordell was the patsy. Donnie John also kept pushing the claim that Turkell was back, having escaped custody, and that the police were covering up that he was still alive.

"One-hundred-thousand-dollar reward for incontrovertible evidence of the Maniac Cop's return!" John shouted at the camera whenever he could.

Most people knew this was a hollow promise. Knew it was fake. Knew that Turkell was dead.

But not Charlie.

He not only believed it, but he also actively tried to film every cop encounter he could, then sent it in, hoping to get the reward. This was now his ninth attempt, and little did he know, his tapes were not even opened by the *Criminals at Large* team anymore, as they all believed he was a crazy fan who just wasted their time.

Charlie slipped out of his apartment and into the night, camera in hand, ducking behind parked cars as he made his way toward the commotion still happening on the other side of the vacant street.

Through the viewfinder, he peered around the side of a car and caught his first glimpse of the scene. A man lay crumpled on the pavement, barely moving. Blood poured from his nose and mouth. Above him, a massive cop loomed, billy club in hand.

Charlie zoomed in. *This is better than the shit before*, he thought.

The club lifted. *This is gold!*

He zoomed out again.

He had not focused on the cop himself. He just saw the man on the ground whimpering and the attack about to happen.

Charlie sucked in a breath. His hands trembled, but he kept rolling. He could stop. He should intervene . . . but one hundred grand was a hundred thousand reasons to just shut up and keep filming.

Then the billy club in the cop's hand twisted apart,

the two halves sliding free to reveal a long, gleaming blade.

Charlie froze. *What?*

The reality of what he saw began to sink in. The fantasy of filming the Maniac Cop in his mind did not include seeing and hearing a defenseless man being killed. He had overlooked that possibility. He didn't know what he thought, nothing except . . . he had to get out of here. He didn't want to film this anymore.

This was him. The one they whispered about.

The real Maniac Cop.

Charlie lowered the camera for a fraction of a second. His pulse pounded against his skull as he tried to look at the man in the burned and moldy uniform. He saw the scars, the open wounds. The many bullet holes.

He then forced himself to look back into the viewfinder. One more shot before I back away and run home.

And then the cop moved.

Not toward his victim.

Toward the lens.

The knife remained poised in the air, but the figure no longer seemed interested in the man at his feet. Instead, his head lifted, his gaze locking directly on the camera.

Charlie held his breath as the world around him tilted.

Stumbling back in a sudden panic, the camera shook in his hands as he turned to run.

Getting to the other side of the street, Charlie stared back and could see the huge cop watching him, not chasing. But before he could turn back around, he slammed into something solid.

Hands clamped onto his shoulders, steadying him as he screamed.

He saw the uniform. A badge. A cop.

"Officer," he gasped. "You gotta help me. You gotta—"

But she wasn't looking past him.

She was looking at him with her terrifying burned, melted, and blistered face.

He looked down at her uniform, scorched, barely clinging to her body.

Her lips never moved. But her hand did.

It shot out, fingers curling around his throat.

Charlie's feet left the ground. His hands flailed, the camera lens shaking as his body convulsed, his windpipe crushed in her grip.

The tape would survive. It would capture it all.

But Charlie would not.

From high up in her and Charlie's apartment, Mae's screams pierced the night. She clutched the window frame as she watched Charlie's body drop to the pavement below. The camera falling beside him, its lens shattering on impact.

She watched in terror as Teresa crossed the road to join Cordell. Without a word, they turned and walked toward the river. The fog rising from the water thickened around them, swallowing them whole.

Moonjean was surprised to see Houngan. The Haitian shaman. Even more surprised was he to see the man looking sheepish as he walked in the room. Sitting down by the bed and talking as he was on the precipice of crying. He had been told by the precinct that he was in this hospital, so the old man came here and waited.

Moonjean stared, watching the old man struggle with his words. He had never seen him like this, hesitant, almost afraid.

The Houngan swallowed hard. "I was the one who raised him," he finally admitted, his voice barely above a whisper. "The man you are looking for, Matthew Cordell . . . I . . . I did it."

Moonjean's face remained unreadable, but inside, his stomach tightened. He had suspected there could be some link to the zombies from his culture, but hearing that the Houngan was behind this, knowing that it wasn't just some unknown force but *him* . . .

The old man sat slumped in the chair beside the hospital bed, his fingers idly gripping the beads around his neck. He looked . . . small. Moonjean had known him in another life, back when his voice carried weight, back when his eyes burned with the intensity of someone who commanded gods. Yet he was just an old man, defeated, broken by something he had unleashed and could not control.

"I thought it would be different," the Houngan continued. His voice was fragile, almost lost beneath the steady beep of the heart monitor beside them. "But the moment he rose . . . I knew something was very wrong. I tried to guide him. But he . . . he just had a lust for death. Any death. He was not empty. He was infected with . . . hate. *So much* hate. And the more I tried to pull him back, to constrain him, the more . . . the more he—" He thought for a moment.

Moonjean exhaled, leaning back into his bed. His wounds throbbed, but he wouldn't let them distract him. "Why?" His voice was low, measured. "Why would you do this?"

The old man's shoulders sagged under the weight of his confession. "Greed . . ." he admitted with a sour chuckle. His fingers wrapped around his beaded necklace nervously. "I wanted his power. I thought—" He inhaled sharply, forcing himself to look at Moonjean. "I thought I could do something no other priest had done. I thought if I could raise a man who had been denied even by the Baron himself, I could . . ." His lips pressed into a thin, grim line.

Moonjean stared. He understood. It was hubris. The Houngan had not been paid to do it, had not been coerced. He had simply believed he was greater than death itself, and he had been wrong.

The Houngan swallowed. "Zombies . . . they exist on fragments. Pieces of who they were. The strongest of them can even speak, obey, exist in this world without falling apart. Yet they are still weak, because there is always a way to reclaim their souls. But Matthew Cordell . . ." He let out a breath, shaking his head. "He did not come back like them. Only his rage did." His eyes flickered to Moonjean's. "No memory. No identity. No humanity. A force, nothing more. His very existence spits in the face of the Baron and the Loa . . . I do not know why they allowed it. You asked me before . . . What if he just came back? Well, I think he did. Before all this. I think that is why this happened. I called on a man who was already empty."

"He gave a load of criminals weapons."

The Houngan didn't know what that meant, but he shrugged. "Cordell is chaos. I saw him kill. Not always everyone. He leaves witnesses. He does things that make no sense, not unless you realize that he is just a force. Not a thought. Like the wind going where it must."

Moonjean inhaled deeply, forcing himself to remain calm. "Then, why did he go after Teresa if he didn't know anything. How is that chaos?"

"The policewoman?" The Houngan's expression darkened. "Because I sent him to her."

Moonjean's fingers clenched the thin hospital sheet beneath him. "You did what?"

The old man's voice wavered. "I thought I could call his soul back to him. I thought if he saw something familiar, if he felt *something* from the past, it would restore his humanity . . . If he saw what happened to the one he hurt . . . I read about her. I knew their connection." He swallowed hard, shaking his head. "But I was wrong. So wrong." His eyes darted down to his shaking hands. "I kept sending him here. Ordering him to watch her . . . But instead of remembering who he was, it only anchored his rage to her. Tethered it to her . . . It did not change his emptiness inside. It did not stop the hate."

A chill passed through Moonjean. "What about the child?"

The Houngan's expression dropped. "The what?"

He didn't know? Moonjean thought. "Teresa Mallory's pregnant. But . . . It had a heartbeat. Even when she didn't."

The old man's lips parted slightly, and for the first time since he entered the room, true fear filled his face. His hands gripped his wooden beads tighter. "No. That . . . that can't be." He inhaled sharply. "So, that was his tether? No . . . No . . ."

The man stood abruptly, pacing the small room as his breathing quickened. "That thing . . . Cordell . . . HE can't father children. He's a corpse. He has no life, no seed to give. That child—" He stopped, staring at

Moonjean as though seeing a ghost. "That child was not created."

"Then what the fuck is it?"

The old man swallowed hard. "In the old tales, there are whispers of this. A new life born not of flesh but of darkness. Of rage . . . It is not a child. It is a manifestation."

"Of what?"

"Of Cordell's hate. And . . . I suppose of the police-woman's longing."

Moonjean blinked. "Teresa's?"

The Houngan nodded solemnly. "She must have wanted a child. Even deep in her subconscious, even while dying. Her desire . . . combined with the unnat-ural presence . . . created . . . something." His fingers gripped his beads tighter. "And those things that are born like this, they are world destroyers. Beyond the evil that a man can create. Something that has never been alive nor dead."

Moonjean had no words.

The Houngan finally exhaled and turned toward the door. "I came here because I wanted to say I am sorry," he muttered. "Before . . . they find me."

"What do you mean?"

"As soon as they united, they came for me. My congregation. Everything. So, I ran . . ." He shook his head. "That didn't stop them. They crossed the city to find me. All those murders on the news . . . It was them killing as they walked in my direction."

Moonjean felt his heart skip. "You brought them here?"

The Houngan nodded. "Yes. But I am not running. Not anymore. I have to pay for my actions now. But I had to tell someone the truth before I leave." His eyes darkened. "Harmony is needed. I took hate from the earth so the earth must be repaid. I cannot give him back to them. But I can offer myself. Maybe it will stop the death. Maybe my death as his creator will mean they can finally take him for good."

Moonjean opened his mouth to argue, but the Houngan just gave him a weak, tired smile.

Then he turned and walked toward his fate.

The corridor on the opposite side of the ward was silent. It was very late, so no one walking the halls, no sounds of people chattering were all the norm. But for the Houngan, the silence said a lot to him. It told him to leave. It warned him. He closed his eyes, ignoring his inner voices screaming at him to leave, and to go back to Haiti. To hide in a place no one would come to look for him. But his better self ignored those voices.

As he walked, he did so carefully, his sandaled feet silently stepping over the cold floor. The further he got down the hallway, the more a sense of dread hung in the air, but something else did, too. Something that he could identify. Something that told him that this was it. He could smell the rancid stench of the risen dead.

Turning a corner, he had to steel himself as, ahead, slumped against the wall, the police guard who had been stationed outside Moonjean's office was sitting grotesquely in his chair. The man's head had been removed and sat on his own lap, looking out. The blood from the body having jetted up through the open neck and soaked the body beneath it. Dripping down and pooling beneath him, congealing in thick, dark patches.

The Houngan had called upon many spirits in his time, danced with the forces of life and death when the mood took him, but none had ever come forth as powerfully as this. What he had risen and what now stalked these halls was beyond anything he had ever dealt with. Beyond anything people should see.

The distant hum of hospital machines filled the silence, the soft beeping of unseen monitors in patients' rooms.

Then, behind him—a sound.

Not footsteps.

Just a foul breath breathing down upon him.

Slowly, fearfully, the Houngan turned to face his demons.

There, as if from nowhere, less than a foot away from him, were his creations.

Cordell, the Maniac Cop, stood like a monolith, his grotesque, burned face stared out from beneath the brim of his moldy cap. Beside him, with just as an unnatural stare, was Teresa. Burned and shot full of holes, she stared at him with eyes that were wide, dead, and knowing.

Neither of them spoke nor did they need to.

The Houngan took a step back, trying to keep his composure.

Cordell did not blink. Did not move.

Teresa's lips parted, but no words came. Only silence.

And then they rushed toward him.

Teresa struck first, her speed inhuman, her hand smashed into the Houngan arms as the bone beneath it cracked. He gasped loudly in pain but had no time to do much else as, with one gloved hand, Cordell swung a monstrous punch that collided with the old man's stomach, sending him flying across the corridor. His body collided with the decapitated security guards, sending them both and the guard's severed head to the floor.

The punch was so great that it crushed the intestines below the skin. A hit that in only a few minutes would be enough to kill the Houngan. But Cordell would not wait. He strode over to the man, and as he passed the guard's head, the Maniac Cop lifted his huge boot and smashed it down on the skull with a terrible roar. Smashing it open in a display of strength.

But the Houngan did not show fear. He tried to stagger to his feet and stand up straight but was too crippled by the punch. He was half hunched as blood seeped from his mouth, his insides heavily bleeding.

Cordell and Teresa were in front of him, ready to exact their violence.

The Houngan, though, did not flinch. He did not beg. His eyes did not show fear or even the pain racking his broken body, only the weight of his resignation. His voice, though ragged, did not waver.

"You are abominations," he rasped, staring into the dead pair's unblinking eyes. "Things that should not walk, shadows that do not belong."

His trembling finger rose, pointing at Cordell.

"You clawed your way from the dirt, not by Bondye's will but by my foolish voice. But you were not a man to raise. You were never a man at all."

Cordell remained silent, staring.

"But I can undo this," he swore. "There is still a price to pay. A debt to settle. The world must be put right."

The Houngan turned his gaze to Teresa. Her eyes, once human, once full of something more, stared back with that same emptiness.

"I tried to make her revive your soul," he confessed, a bitter realization creeping into his voice. His knees threatened to buckle, but he remained upright. "But your evil infected her."

His vision started to waver, but he spoke stronger, standing a bit more upright. Ignoring the pain. "Baron Samedi, Lord of the Cemetery, hear me now." His voice carried down the corridor, cutting through the still air. "I give you my life. My flesh. My soul. I offer myself in exchange for these two cursed spirits. Take them. Let them rest. Let the earth claim them as you intended."

The silence fell over them.

A deep, stretching silence, as though the very world was listening.

The Houngan smiled victoriously, waiting for the Baron to appear.

He waited.

And then . . . nothing.

His lips parted slightly, waiting for the shift in the air, the rush of divine power, the answer.

Nothing.

His eyes flickered upward. He had expected something—a whisper on the wind, a tremor in the earth, the unseen weight of judgment.

Nothing came.

A flicker of doubt crept into his face.

Even a cursed thing could be reclaimed. Even a monster could be called back.

Balance must always be restored. That is the law. *Wasn't it?*

He had been ready to die. Ready to give everything —because that is how it had always been.

But now?

A realization crashed into the old man. "No . . ." he whispered.

His eyes darted toward Cordell, realization striking like lightning.

It was never about a soul.

It was never about balance.

He had never been part of the equation at all.

His sacrifice was meaningless.

Not because it failed.

But because it was never even considered.

The gods had not forsaken him.

They had simply never been listening.

The Houngan let out a breath. And then . . . he laughed, a soft, bitter sound.

"I raised a thing that even the gods cannot touch . . ." he whispered. His smile was small, his final act one of faith—even if that faith had failed him.

Cordell raised his hand and brought it down like a hammer.

The impact shattered the Houngan's skull with a sickening crack. If the ruined stomach wound had not signed his death warrant, the broken spine and collapsed skull did. His body convulsed, his last moments spent in violent spasms, his life spilling across the hospital floor.

And in that final moment—his dying breath wasn't a prayer.

It was understanding.

Even his gods had no dominion here.

Detective Moonjean lay in his hospital bed, unable to move, unable to get up. The plaster casts, together with his injuries, forced him down onto the bed, rendering him helpless.

And all he could do after the Houngan left his room was listen.

It started as a dull thud.

Then the noises began. The scream. The roar. The crash. The loud voice of the defiant Houngan.

Moonjean knew what was happening and could not do a thing to stop it. He glanced around the room, desperate to find something that could save him. A hiding place. A weapon.

The noise soon stopped.

And then came footsteps.

Moonjean started to sweat, fearing what was coming. But then the footsteps changed. They were not the heavy, measured steps of Cordell but frantic, racing toward him.

Through the half-open door to the corridor, Naomi suddenly appeared, panicked.

"Quick!" she screamed. "We gotta go now! The hospital is in evacuation. They're here!"

She ran over to the bed. Without even looking at him, she went around to all four wheels and released the brake clamps on each one.

Getting to the rear of it, she then pushed the bed out. It glided easily on the wheels as she forced it toward the corridor.

"Where are we going?" Moonjean asked.

Naomi just pushed the bed out into the corridor

and turned in the opposite direction of where the Houngan had gone.

As she wheeled the bed down the brightly lit hallway, they quickly approached the nurses' station. It was abandoned. Above it, the red emergency light flickered silently.

Everywhere around them was empty. They were the last ones on this ward.

The elevator dinged, stealing their attention.

Wheeling the bed over to them, they soon came to a sudden halt.

The doors in front of them had been stuck open, stuttering slightly as they attempted to close, only to be jammed by what remained of a nurse's body. Her severed leg lay wedged between the metal, the flesh mangled and twisted as the doors tried to shut.

Blood soaked the floor in a dark pool as the rest of her body parts lay in a decimated heap.

The elevator dinged again.

Naomi quickly turned the bed back down the corridor and continued, pushing faster away from the scene with more urgency. The bed's wheels squeaked in a rhythmic beat as she sped away.

On the bed, Moonjean twisted to meet her gaze. "Get me out of this," he pleaded urgently. "I can walk . . . I can do it."

She didn't answer. Didn't even look at him. She just kept on pushing as hard as she could manage.

The service elevators. They were her only chance.

They were through the next three wards, on the far side of the hospital. If she could get them there, they might have a way out.

The building stretched ahead in endless corridors, twisting through bright fluorescent lights. Naomi barreled the bed forward, shoving through swinging doors, weaving through the turning paths.

Still, no one was around. No patients. No staff. All had evacuated.

Moonjean had no choice but to lay still. He could do nothing but witness.

Chapter 9

The service elevators lay at the far end of the maintenance corridor, beyond the pediatrics ward. Where the ward, even at night, would usually be rife with the sounds of occasional cries from the young, the only noise was the repeating squeak of the hospital bed's wheels as it passed through and up to the large elevator doors.

Naomi, exhausted, rushed around the bed and hit the call button on the wall. Turning back to Moonjean, she offered a slight smile of comfort. "It'll be over soon. One quick ride down, and we're out by the exit."

The elevator door immediately slid open, screeching. With a relieved exhalation, Naomi pushed Moonjean's bed forward, halfway into the elevator.

A gasp caught in her throat the instant she realized what had happened. Instead of the sturdy floor of the elevator, only deep darkness stretched out beneath the bed's wheels. A rush of cold air blew out from the open shaft, carrying with it the smell of oiled machinery. Instinctively, every muscle in her body tensed as she suddenly gripped the rails to keep Moonjean from rolling in any further. But he was heavy as was the metal frame.

No matter how hard she tried to pull, the front wheels of the bed hooked over the rim at the bottom of the elevator door, the weight pushing the end down too far. She pushed down on the bed with all of her might, but it kept slipping in.

Moonjean, barely lucid in his pained exhaustion, let out a small, confused whimper, one that trailed off into silence the moment he peered over the edge of the bed. His attention was then ripped upward as somewhere above in the shadows, the elevator's faint rumble sounded.

"Naomi?" he managed to utter as he saw the large metal base of the elevator descending out of the high darkness. "Pull me out now!"

She felt her stomach drop as she heard the noise, too—the low, metallic rumble of gears getting louder and louder. There was no time to wonder why the elevator had suddenly sprung to life again or how the door had even opened, only the horrifying certainty that its approach meant destruction. She braced her feet and heaved, trying once more in vain to free the front wheels of the bed from where they snagged on the open shaft. The metal frame just refused to budge. It groaned in protest, half-suspended in midair.

"You have to crawl over to me!" she screamed, admitting that she didn't have the strength to save him.

Moonjean, sprawled on the bed, stared up with wide, fearful eyes. The growing clatter of chains and gears grew louder. The elevator was closer.

"NOW!" she screamed at him again. "I can't hold on!"

In a burst of terrified desperation, he threw his weight backward and screamed in pain as he climbed back over the bed's railing. His fractured hip sent fire through his nerves as he used his good arm to pull himself over the head bar toward her.

As he came within grabbing distance, Naomi let go of the bed and grabbed onto Moonjean, dragging him back to the floor just as the service elevator arrived. The force of it twisted and snapped the metal frame in an earsplitting wail. Sparks flew as metal pressed against metal, the elevator trying to make its way past the crumpled blockage. Then, with a sudden shriek of gears and an explosion from the motor, the elevator sputtered as it stalled, unable to carry on its descent.

For a moment, all Naomi could do was stare at the bed, crumpled and pinned beneath the elevator. Then she glimpsed Moonjean curled on the floor a few steps away, grimacing in pain, holding his hip as tears dripped down from the corners of his squeezed-shut eyes. She scrambled to his side as he lay trembling from head to toe.

Still, despite this, he forced out a pained grin. "I told you . . . I'd walk."

Naomi let out a small laugh of relief, reaching for Moonjean's one good hand and helping him to his feet. "Hang on to me," she murmured urgently, putting an arm around his torso, ensuring she took all the weight off his hip. "Just put your weight on me."

Having no other option but to lean heavily on her, Moonjean managed to stand, despite the agony.

"Where do we go?" he asked.

"Only one choice." She nodded down the corridor. "The old wing is that way. We gotta make our way down from there."

Together, they staggered away from the ruined elevator, limping down the corridor toward a pair of boarded-up double doors marked with a glaring red sign: *Danger*.

The old hospital wing lay beyond, but it was not a safe place. It had been sealed off with wooden planks, slated for demolition in the coming months.

"You gotta stand on your own for a second, okay? I gotta get the door."

Nodding, he slowly shifted his weight and, with a painful gasp, leaned against the wall. The pain burned, but he forced his body not to give up.

Naomi, mustering whatever strength she had left, started prying at the nail-ridden planks. They were surprisingly easy to pull off the frame. Where the nails didn't slide out, the wood was not too thick to snap off.

Within minutes, they had slipped into the darkness of the condemned wing, Moonjean back to using Naomi as a prop to walk.

After a painful, slow walk down the staircase, they came out into a large, half-demolished section of the old hospital wing. A room open to the elements on the second floor. It was a ghostly place, made more eerie by the silver moonlight drifting in through the missing section of the roof. If a bomb had gone off right then, it could not have left the structure in more disarray. The wrecking ball had reduced walls to wreckage, and the remaining floorboards threatened to collapse under any weight.

Moonjean stepped gingerly, barefoot and unsteady, wincing each time he placed his foot on the ground. The debris all over the floor dug into his flesh, but he refused to stop.

Naomi walked beside him, taking his weight. "We're nearly there," she told him softly.

They soon crossed the room and reached a section where something was missing, the staircase to the ground floor. At the spot where it once stood, all that remained was sheer drop-down. The steps had been torn out. They stared into this empty space where their escape should have been.

"We gotta climb down," Moonjean said, not sounding strong enough to speak, let alone descend a wrecked building. But he was not giving in just because of his injuries. He quickly reached for a nearby beam to take the weight off Naomi, but almost immediately, it gave way beneath his grip, nearly taking him over the edge into the missing staircase. Only Naomi's steadying hand kept him from stumbling.

"No, this way," Naomi said, nodding toward the other side of the room. "There's gotta be a fire escape."

With no electrical power left in the wing, the moonlight breaking through the missing parts of the building was their sole guide. They slowly hobbled back across the room, navigating through the remains of a leveled corridor under beams and twisted metal.

As they neared the far wall, a massive concrete pillar stood in their path, barely discernible in the dim light. They moved toward it carefully, hoping to skirt around its base.

Then something stepped out from behind it . . .

A tall, ominous shape coalesced from the darkness. A silent presence that, in an instant, towered over them.

It was Cordell.

In an instant, he had Moonjean by the throat, but the detective wasn't going down without a fight. Using the heavy plaster cast on his arm, he battered the Maniac Cop across the side of the head. Not just once. He drew his arm back again and again, smashing it into

Cordell. The pain in his arm was secondary to his panic and desperation to get away.

Naomi stumbled back, searching for something to use as a weapon, and walked directly into the path of Teresa, who advanced speedily from the shadows.

As Moonjean was slowly strangled to death by Cordell's huge gloved hands, he gasped for breath. His plaster cast beating had no effect. It just made Cordell tighten his grip.

Despite his struggle, Moonjean stared into Cordell's eyes—one bulging, one sunken. He searched for some semblance of humanity. *Something*. But there was nothing. It was the gaze of a shark. Dark and unreadable.

Naomi, meanwhile, could find nothing to help her fight off Teresa. No pieces of wood or metal she could fashion into a weapon.

"Please," she said desperately, trying to reason with Teresa as she got nearer. "You looked at me once, remember? In your room. You saw me. I told everyone that you were alive in there. I saved you . . ."

But Teresa just drew closer, still silent. Her eyes wide and stern as Naomi continued.

"Just like now. I know you're in there, Teresa. I know you can hear me. You were a cop. A police officer. Moonjean told me . . . You gave everything to stop Cordell from killing. You gave your life. He's the one that killed you, yet you're on his side?"

Behind them, Moonjean began to slump in Cordell's grip, fighting to remain conscious.

Naomi turned back to Teresa. "Moonjean was your friend," she said, her voice rising. "You can save him. You're the only one who can. Do you hear me, Teresa . . . Officer Mallory?"

Teresa suddenly slowed. Something seemed to stir in her as her wide eyes narrowed. The words Officer Mallory triggered a faint recognition. The burned officer hesitated. She stared at Naomi, then moved her gaze over her shoulder to Cordell.

She remembered . . . Her thoughts were not as empty as Cordell's. From the fog of her rage came the sound of a chainsaw. Rattling violently. She could feel its frenetic vibrations in her hand as she held it up to . . . to the Maniac Cop. Then Cordell's grip around her waist. The snap of bones. She remembered being murdered and could feel every snap of her body again.

Naomi screamed out again, louder. "You can't become like him. You're good! You were a good person."

In a burst of sudden motion, Teresa lashed out, knocking Naomi to one side. At first, it appeared as though she meant to attack. Instead, she rushed past Naomi and bounded toward Cordell, a snarl creeping over her melted face.

Cordell was about to end Moonjean entirely when Teresa came up behind him and seized the billy club hanging from his belt. She twisted it free, revealing the stiletto hidden inside. Cordell turned his head in surprise but was too preoccupied to react.

Teresa raised the weapon overhead, both hands wrapped around the hilt, then drove the blade into Cordell's back. It did not have the effect a normal blade should. His own weapon did something no other had—it caused him pain. Intense, terrible pain.

He let out a cry as he loosened his grip on Moonjean. The wounded detective collapsed among the rubble, coughing and clutching his neck. Cordell turned, swinging a hand at Teresa, but she struck him again.

The blade pierced him in the chest, beside his badge. She pulled it back out and struck again. And again. No blood welled from his wounds, only a strange glow pulsing from within.

He went to hit her again but halted mid-swing. He stared at Teresa with utter disbelief. She was no longer the part of him who shared the path of chaos. If he had any memory of his past left, he would have recognized that look on her face. The same look she had before, when she ran at him with a chainsaw, battling for her life.

No trace of the Maniac Cop remained in her expression nor was there any of who Teresa once was. It was only vengeance. She remembered what he stole from her. Her life.

She stabbed again, deep into his heart, and he staggered. He took several unsteady steps toward her, reaching for her midsection. Some plea shimmered in his gaze, a last demand for mercy on the life she carried. But her response came quickly and without hesitation. She raised the blade again and drove it into his skull.

The impact shook through the rotting floorboards. Then, with a splintering crack, the boards gave way beneath his weight.

Desperation filled him as he lunged for her arm, clutching it in a final bid for survival. Or perhaps it was a desire not to be alone. He may have had no mind left, but like any wild animal, he knew when his time was up. With the emergence of pain back into his dead body and the burning heat inside him, he could see his countdown running out.

Together, they plunged into the darkness below, disappearing through clouds of dust and collapsing timbers. Bits of shattered plaster rained down around them, showering the void with debris.

They crashed onto the next level with meteoric force. Cordell's body struck first, his torso impaled by jagged wood, the sharpened edges splitting through his uniform. In the same heartbeat, Teresa landed against his chest, the same splinters piercing her as well.

Neither the agony nor the shock slowed her. Her eyes were fixed on him. With both hands wrapped around the stiletto, she drove it into him yet again and did not stop. Each strike seemed to open a doorway of pale light within his wounds as though she was punishing something far beyond his flesh.

He tried to raise a hand, tried to form a wordless protest at this betrayal, but her assault did not cease. The timbers beneath them strained under their combined weight, groaning as the broken structure finally surrendered. A new fracture split through the floor, and an instant later, they fell again.

They dropped, vanishing deeper into the ruined sublevels of the old hospital. Timbers snapped and twisted in the gloom as their bodies caught against them. The glimmer that leaked from Cordell's ravaged body flickered in the darkness until the final surge of splintered debris swept them both away into silence.

Deep below, in the stillness following their fall, the rushing of water could be heard.

Back on the second floor, Naomi was down by the collapsed, gasping Moonjean.

"Don't speak . . . Just lie still."

Moonjean looked at her in confusion. "Did you see it?" he spoke in strangled words. "The light from him?"

Naomi nodded but was more concerned with his injuries. "Can you stand? We have to go now. They might come back . . ."

They had no choice.

They had to try to get out.

. . .

By the next morning, a swarm of officers spread out across the collapsed wing, peering under jagged slabs of concrete and shifting the remnants of broken beams. Throughout the hospital, workers busied themselves clearing away bodies and returning evacuated patients to their rooms.

Beyond the hospital's perimeter fence, a crowd of neighborhood residents, gang members, junkies, and the homeless looked on. Tension and curiosity briefly united them in the face of recent horrors.

Farther down the street, a pair of fire engines finally got the blaze at the church under control.

The officers moved through heaps of debris, calling out whenever they uncovered anything that might confirm the fate of those responsible. Fear dwelled in their every move. No one felt sure the danger was truly gone.

Next to the parked ambulances, Moonjean sat in a wheelchair, Naomi standing by his side. Both wore grim expressions as they silently observed the officers, who grew more discouraged with each fruitless hour of searching. He could even see the priest, Father Paul, helping out in the search.

"No sign up here!" one officer shouted.

Another, emerging from a gap in the foundation, ran a dusty hand through his hair. "Nothing but a crack leading to some old sewer lines. Think they could've got out through there?"

"Keep looking. We'll find something," someone

replied, though every word felt more hollow than the last.

Eventually, Naomi guided Moonjean back from the wreckage. No further discoveries would be made that day. No remains would ever be found. Officer Matthew Cordell and Officer Teresa Mallory had vanished, leaving only a lingering unease.

Eight months later . . .

Massive construction was underway on the site where the old hospital wing had once stood. A towering fence enclosed the area, bearing a bold sign: *Site of the new Queen of Mercy Hospital, Children's Wing, Consolidated Mutual Construction Corporation.*

Not so long ago, the ground beyond the fence had been littered with the remains of a collapsed building. Since then, with heavy equipment parked in neat rows and new concrete foundations taking shape, a modern structure had begun to rise. It promised a fresh start for this part of the city, perhaps marking the first step toward reclaiming a neighborhood that had fallen into neglect.

Dawn light cast its long shadow across the site. Work had not yet begun for the day; the crews were absent, and the night watchman nowhere in sight.

Still, there was movement within its half-finished steel skeletal frame. An elderly homeless woman in her seventies picked her way through the construction zone. She carried several plastic bags and paused whenever she spotted anything left behind by the workers, scraps of food, dented soda cans, or empty bottles. Anything she could drink, collect or sell.

Her progress led her deeper into the maze of girders and piled-up bricks. She was tired. Weary from the days of continual struggle on the streets. The tattered clothing she wore revealed a rough existence, and she moved carefully across the uneven ground. She did not know how much longer she could live this, but she would not quit today. Today, she would survive.

Then, a faint cry drifted toward her from below.

The sound then came again.

Unmistakably, it was an infant's wail.

She followed it, scanning the discarded materials and half-buried cement blocks.

She stopped in her tracks as she lowered the bags to the ground.

"Now, where in hell did you come from?" she asked with a joy in her voice.

There, down a large slope, among the debris and building materials, was a small child, a newborn. Filthy, naked, and trembling.

Taking off a frayed scarf from her neck, the old lady started to walk down the slope to the baby.

As she hobbled away, leaving her bags behind her, swaddling the infant in her scarves, its cries followed, lingering, even when she disappeared from view.

Also by Christian Francis

Official Novelizations

Session 9: The Official Novelization

978-1-916582-59-0 (eBook)

978-1-916582-60-6 (Paperback)

978-1-916582-61-3 (Hardcover)

Released October 2024

★★★★★

"This book was a WILD ride. I was literally biting my nails while getting through it!"

Skylere K (Netgalley)

The First Power: The Official Novelization

978-1-916582-95-8 (eBook)

978-1-916582-66-8 (Paperback)

978-1-916582-67-5 (Hardcover)

Released April 2025

Maniac Cop

978-1-916582-68-2 (eBook)

978-1-916582-70-5 (Paperback)

Released May 20 2025

Maniac Cop 2

978-1-916582-71-2 (eBook)

978-1-916582-73-6 (Paperback)

Released May 20 2025

Maniac Cop 3

978-1-916582-74-3 (eBook)

978-1-916582-76-7 (Paperback)

Released May 20 2025

Maniac Cop Trilogy

978-1-916582-69-9 (Hardcover)

978-1-916582-72-9 (Mass Market Paperback)

Released May 20 2025

From Echo On Publications

- The Gate (*coming soon*)
- Dee Snider's Strangeland (*coming soon*)
- 3615 Code Père Noël aka Deadly Games (*coming soon*)
- In The Mouth of Madness (*coming soon*)

plus many more to be announced.

From Titan Publishing Group

- The Descent (*coming soon*)

From Encyclopocalypse Publications

- Wishmaster
- Vamp
- Creature, aka Titan Find

Original Novels and Novellas

The Dead Woods

YA Horror

978-1-916582-00-2 (eBook)

978-1-916582-02-6 (Paperback)

978-1-916582-04-0 (Hardcover)

"One of the best YA books I have ever read."

David W Adams (Amazon)

———

The Devil and The Deep

Cosmic Horror

978-1-916582-52-1 (eBook)

978-1-916582-55-2 (Paperback)

978-1-916582-54-5 (Hardcover)

The Sacrifice of Anton Stacey

Horror Novella

978-1-916582-06-4 (eBook)

979-8-386183-59-2 (Paperback)

———

Everyday Monsters - The Animus Chronicles 1

Dark Fantasy / Horror

978-1-916582-03-3 (eBook)

978-1-916582-09-5 (Paperback)

978-1-916582-10-1 (Hardcover)

———

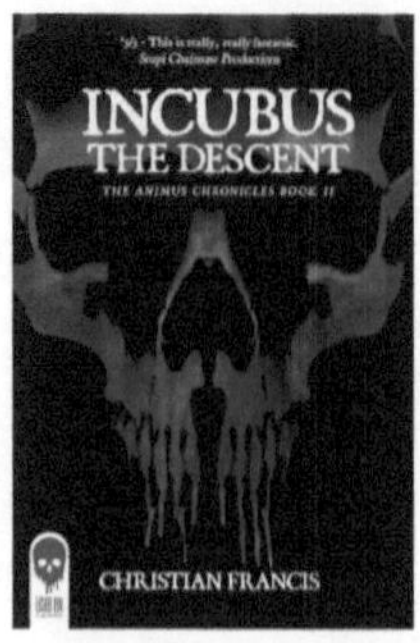

Incubus: The Descent - The Animus Chronicles 2

Dark Fantasy / Horror

978-1-916582-08-8 (eBook)

978-1-916582-11-8 (Paperback)

978-1-916582-12-5 (Hardcover)

Anti Rule: Navigating The Lies About Fiction Writing

Non-Fiction

978-1-916582-01-9 (eBook)

978-1-916582-05-7 (Paperback)

www.ingramcontent.com/pod-product-compliance
Lightning Source LLC
Chambersburg PA
CBHW060551190726
48283CB00003B/966